# HARLEQUIN®
## Presents~

Harlequin Presents never fails to bring you the most gorgeous, brooding alpha heroes—so don't miss out on this month's irresistible collection!

THE ROYAL HOUSE OF NIROLI series continues with Susan Stephens's *Expecting His Royal Baby*. The king has found provocative prince Nico Fierezza a suitable bride. But Carrie has been in love with Nico—her boss—for years, and after one night of passion is pregnant!

When handsome Peter Ramsey discovers Erin's having his baby in *The Billionaire's Captive Bride* by Emma Darcy, he offers her the only thing he can think of to guarantee his child's security—marriage! In *The Greek Tycoon's Unwilling Wife* by Kate Walker, Andreas has lost his memory, but what will happen when he recalls throwing Rebecca out of his house on their wedding day—for reasons only he knows? If you're feeling festive, you'll love *The Boss's Christmas Baby* by Trish Morey, where a boss discovers his convenient mistress is expecting his baby. In *The Spanish Duke's Virgin Bride* by Chantelle Shaw, ruthless Spanish billionaire Duke Javier Herrera sees in Grace an opportunity for revenge *and* a contract wife! In *The Italian's Pregnant Mistress* by Cathy Williams, millionaire Angelo Falcone has Francesca in his power and in his bed, and this time he won't let her go. In *Contracted: A Wife for the Bedroom* by Carol Marinelli, Lily knows Hunter's ring will only be on her finger for twelve months, but soon a year doesn't seem long enough! Finally, brand-new author Susanne James brings you *Jed Hunter's Reluctant Bride*, where Jed demands Cryssie marry him because it makes good business sense, but Cryssie's feelings run deeper.... Enjoy!

**Harlequin Presents®**

**GREEK TYCOONS**

They're the men who have everything—
except brides...

Wealth, power, charm—what else could
a heart-stoppingly handsome tycoon need?
In the GREEK TYCOONS miniseries you have
already been introduced to some gorgeous
Greek multimillionaires who are in need of wives.

Now it's the turn of popular Presents author
Kate Walker, with her attention-grabbing romance
*The Greek Tycoon's Unwilling Wife*.

This tycoon has met his match, and he's decided
he *has* to have her...*whatever* that takes!

# Kate Walker

# THE GREEK TYCOON'S UNWILLING WIFE

GREEK
TYCOONS

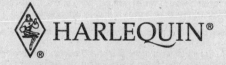

HARLEQUIN®

TORONTO • NEW YORK • LONDON
AMSTERDAM • PARIS • SYDNEY • HAMBURG
STOCKHOLM • ATHENS • TOKYO • MILAN • MADRID
PRAGUE • WARSAW • BUDAPEST • AUCKLAND

If you purchased this book without a cover you should be aware that this book is stolen property. It was reported as "unsold and destroyed" to the publisher, and neither the author nor the publisher has received any payment for this "stripped book."

ISBN-13: 978-0-373-12677-4
ISBN-10:     0-373-12677-8

THE GREEK TYCOON'S UNWILLING WIFE

First North American Publication 2007.

Copyright © 2007 by Kate Walker.

All rights reserved. Except for use in any review, the reproduction or utilization of this work in whole or in part in any form by any electronic, mechanical or other means, now known or hereafter invented, including xerography, photocopying and recording, or in any information storage or retrieval system, is forbidden without the written permission of the publisher, Harlequin Enterprises Limited, 225 Duncan Mill Road, Don Mills, Ontario, Canada M3B 3K9.

This is a work of fiction. Names, characters, places and incidents are either the product of the author's imagination or are used fictitiously, and any resemblance to actual persons, living or dead, business establishments, events or locales is entirely coincidental.

This edition published by arrangement with Harlequin Books S.A.

® and TM are trademarks of the publisher. Trademarks indicated with ® are registered in the United States Patent and Trademark Office, the Canadian Trade Marks Office and in other countries.

www.eHarlequin.com

**Printed in U.S.A.**

**All about the author...**
*Kate Walker*

KATE WALKER was born in Nottinghamshire, England, and was the middle child in a family of five girls. She grew up in a home where books were vitally important, and she read anything she could get her hands on. Even before she could write she was making up stories. She can't remember a time when she wasn't scribbling away at something. But everyone told her she would never make a living as a writer, so she decided if she couldn't write books, at least she could work with them by becoming a librarian.

It was at the University College of Wales, Aberystwyth, that she met her husband, who was also studying at the college. They married and eventually moved to Lincolnshire, where she worked as a children's librarian until her son was born.

After three years of being a full-time housewife and mother she was ready for a new challenge, but needed something she could do at home. So she turned to her old love of writing. The first two novels she sent off to Harlequin were rejected, but the third attempt was successful. She can still remember the moment a letter of acceptance arrived instead of the rejection slip she had been dreading. But the moment she really realized she was a published writer was when copies of her first book, *The Chalk Line*, arrived just in time to be one of her best Christmas presents ever.

Kate is often asked if she's a romantic person, because she writes romances. Her answer is that if being romantic means caring about other people enough to make that extra-special effort for them, then yes, she is.

Kate loves to hear from her fans. You can contact her through her website at www.kate-walker.com, or e-mail her at: kate@kate-walker.com.

For Michelle Reid.

A great writer, a great friend, whose support and whip-cracking was invaluable to me as I wrote this.

# CHAPTER ONE

THE villa looked just as she remembered it.

Or rather, Rebecca acknowledged to herself, it looked just as it had always appeared in her dreams. Because the truth was that she had actually seen so very little of it on that one day she had ever spent inside it.

The one day that should have been the start of her honeymoon.

The one day of her marriage.

They had arrived just as the sun was setting and so she had only had the briefest glimpse of the huge, elegant, white-painted building, the sweep of the bay behind it blue and crystal-clear. But it seemed that that had been enough to etch the image onto her mind with perfect clarity so that the memories that had surfaced in her sleep were far more detailed and accurate than she would ever have imagined she could describe when awake.

Clearly the eyes of happiness recorded things much better than vision that was blurred and distorted by tears. Because that was how she remembered her arrival at the Villa Aristea, and then, just a few short hours later, her departure from it. She had reached the tiny island in the heights of delirious happiness, and left it just a few short hours later in the very depths of despair.

She hadn't even had time to unpack her case. Rebecca shivered in spite of the heat of the sun on her back as she recalled the way that Andreas had picked it up and flung it out of the door in a blazing, black rage. She had been so sure that he would have flung her out after it that she hadn't stayed even to protest, but had fled in a rush, trying to convince herself that discretion was the better part of valour and that she would do better to wait until he'd calmed down before she tried to explain the truth. At least then she might have a hope that he would listen.

She'd waited. And waited. But it had seemed that Andreas would never, ever calm down at all.

Until now.

'Is this the right place, *kyria*?'

Behind her, on the steep, curving road, the taxi driver stirred restlessly in the afternoon heat. He was clearly anxious to get back to the tiny village and into the shade once again.

'Oh, yes,' Rebecca assured him hastily, opening her bag and rooting in it awkwardly, hunting for her purse and thumbing through the unfamiliar notes she'd acquired in a rush at the very last minute, hunting for one that looked something like the amount on the meter. 'Yes, this is the right place.'

It was impossible not to contrast the shambles and discomfort of her arrival today with the way she had first visited the Villa Aristea barely a year before. Then she had travelled in the greatest possible comfort, flying to Rhodes in Andreas' private jet and then being ferried in a helicopter across the sea to this island that was little more than a dot in the ocean.

And she hadn't had to lift a finger. Everything had been arranged for her. Everything planned to be the end of a perfect day and the start of a perfect marriage.

Except, of course, it hadn't worked out at all that way. That day had been the start of nothing and had brought the end of her ill-fated marriage before it had even really begun.

Except in one way…

Bitter tears burned at the backs of her eyes as she was forced to remember how Andreas had so ruthlessly made sure that their marriage could not be dissolved easily and swiftly.

'There will be no annulment,' he had declared coldly and harshly, making it plain that that was what had been at the back of his mind all the time. He hadn't wanted her for himself any more, but he had made so sure that she could not be with anyone else for as long as he could keep her from it. 'If you want your freedom, you will have to go through the full legal procedure.'

'*If* I want my freedom!' Rebecca had flung at him, blinded by pain and desperate to get out of there before she had broken down and let him see just what he had done to her. '*If*! I wouldn't come back to you if you crawled over broken glass to come to me to beg for my return.'

He'd tossed aside her furious protest with an indifferent shrug of one powerful shoulder, a look of scorn on his beautiful face.

'You'll come crawling to me before I ever even think of you, if only because you need money for something. I'll be willing to bet that you'll come looking for cash before the year is up.'

'Never…' Rebecca had begun, desperate to stop him from thinking of her like this. 'I'd rather die.'

He'd scorned that declaration too, swatting it away as if her fury were just a buzzing fly that had annoyed him.

'You'll be back—because you can't help yourself. You'll want to get your greedy, grasping hands on as much as you can before our marriage is finally over and done with.'

'*Kyria...*'

The taxi driver was still hovering, trying to give her change, it seemed.

'Oh, no...'

Rebecca waved him away, trying to find the strength to smile in spite of her memories.

'Keep it. Keep the change.'

She might need him later, she told herself. Sooner, rather than later, if this interview didn't go well. But certainly at some point soon, she would need a taxi to take her back down to the ferry and it was as well to keep this man friendly as it seemed that he ran the only firm on this island.

She barely heard his thanks or the roar of the car's engine as it swung out into the road and set off down the hill again. Her gaze had gone back to the big, carved wooden door before her and her thoughts to the night, a year ago, when she had crept away from this place like a beaten dog, with her tail well and truly between her legs.

'You'll come crawling to me before I ever even think of you...'

The brutal words echoed again and again inside her mind, making her head ache, and her thoughts blur. She had come crawling to him in desperation, because only desperation could drive her to fulfil his prediction, make the callous words come true when she had vowed that it was the last thing on earth that she would ever want. And she *was* desperate.

But desperation wasn't why she was here.

The terrible news about her baby niece had driven her to write that letter to Andreas, expecting only ever to receive the curtest of replies from him—if in fact he replied at all. She hoped for, prayed for a cheque that would help them out of the terrible fix they were in—a cheque that she had promised him that she would pay back if it was the last thing she did. But she had definitely not dared to hope for anything else.

Certainly she hadn't dared to hope that he would actually see her, or speak to her. Let her put her case in person.

And of course he hadn't.

The formal letter had come almost by return of post.

She was asked to meet with his lawyer. To state exactly why she needed the money and on what terms. And when he had the details then Mr Petrakos would consider her request.

She had been still reeling from the curt coldness of the single typewritten sheet when the telephone had rung.

'Andreas…'

For the first time in almost twelve months Rebecca had let his name slip past her lips, whispering it aloud in the still, hot air, silent except for the buzz of insects amongst the flowers.

She hadn't even been able to say it when she had heard the unknown, accented voice at the other end of the phone ask to speak to Mrs Petrakos. In fact it had taken the space of several stunned heartbeats to even remember that Mrs Petrakos was her own name. She had gone back to using her maiden name after the brutally abrupt end to her marriage and had tried in all ways possible to put the fact that she had ever been Rebecca Petrakos, however briefly, out of her mind for good.

'Come on, Rebecca, *do something*!'

She spoke the words out loud, striving to push herself into action instead of standing there, foolishly, frozen to the spot. She seemed incapable of movement now that she was actually here.

She'd moved fast enough when she'd finally absorbed the phone message from Andreas' PA. Just to know that her husband had had an accident had been bad enough. At the words 'car crash', her blood had run cold, making her shiver in shock as the terrible truth hit home.

A devastating crash. His car brakes had failed and he'd gone off the road, into a tree. He was lucky to still be alive. But he had escaped, though badly battered and bruised—and now he was asking for her.

*Asking for her.*

As they had done back home, those words now pushed Rebecca into action, taking her towards the door, her hand lifting to tug at the ornate bell pull that hung beside it, hearing the sound jangle loudly deep inside the house.

Andreas had been asking for her, the voice at the other end of the phone had said. Did she think she could come to Greece? Would it be possible for her to come to see him?

Becca hadn't needed to *think*. There had been no doubt at all in her mind and she had given her answer even before she had time to consider whether it was wise or not. But the truth was she didn't care.

Andreas had been in a crash, he was hurt—injured—and he was asking for her. She had barely put the phone down before she had dashed upstairs to start packing.

Of course, the journey to Greece had given her too much time to think. Time to go over and over and over the conversation in her head and find all sorts of possible things to worry about and fret over.

What had happened in the accident and how badly hurt was Andreas? Why did he want to speak to her when for almost a year he had kept his distance, maintaining a total silence, with no contact at all, apart from that single stiffly formal letter that she knew he had got his secretary to write and had simply scrawled his name at the bottom of?

But it had been enough to know that Andreas had asked for her. And there was no way she was going to turn her back on him.

She was so absorbed in her thoughts that she barely noticed the big door swing open and jumped, startled, when a voice exclaimed in surprise.

'*Kyria* Petrakos!'

It was Medora, the elderly housekeeper who Andreas had said was the closest he had ever had to a mother. Medora, who had been the one person she had spoken to on that terrible day she had spent at the villa, before Andreas had so unceremoniously thrown her out. The one person who had had a smile for her then and still had now, it seemed.

'Welcome! Come in! The master will be so happy to see you.'

Would he? a little, niggling voice questioned in the back of Becca's thoughts. Would Andreas truly be glad to see her? She had started out on this journey so determined and full of confidence, but somehow along the way all of that courage had seeped away.

What if it had all been a terrible mistake? If Andreas had not been asking for her at all but for someone else? Or what if…?

Her heart clenched at the thought of the possibility that Andreas had asked for her all right but that he had done so for reasons that were far from kind or even friendly. What if his motives were simply to add to the misery he had heaped on her a year ago?

'*Kyria* Petrakos?'

Another voice, a male one this time—the voice from the telephone call—broke into her thoughts, making her turn, blinking hard in the shadowy hallway after the brilliance of the sun outside. A young man, tall, dark, was holding out his hand to her.

'My name is Leander Gazonas. I work for *Kyrie* Petrakos. It was I who telephoned you.'

Leander's handclasp was warm and firm, reassuringly so.

It drove away some of the doubts and fears in Becca's thoughts, and replaced them with new confidence and hope.

'Thank you for getting in touch with me. I came as soon as I could.'

'So would you like a drink—or a chance to freshen up? Medora will show you to your room.'

If a room had been put at her disposal then it seemed that, for the moment at least, Andreas was not just going to turn round and reject her again. But where was Andreas himself? How was he?

'If it's all right, I'd like to see my…'

The word died on her tongue and she found herself unable to actually say 'my husband' out loud.

'I'd like to see Mr Petrakos, if that's possible.'

If there was anything that brought home to her just how ambiguous her presence here was, it was this. The way that she was standing here, in the hallway of the home of the man who was, legally at least, her husband, waiting for an invitation to move into the house, while somewhere else in the building Andreas, the man she had promised to love, honour and cherish—and who had made the same vow to her—was…

Was what? Why was she being kept here, waiting like this? What had happened to Andreas? Where was he? Something about the look in Leander's eyes made panic rise in her throat.

'Is my husband all right? Where is he? How is he?'

'Please don't upset yourself, Mrs Petrakos.'

The tone was soothing, obviously meant to calm, but still there was something about the man's expression, his careful control of his words that set her nerves on edge. It was obvious that there was something he was holding back.

'Your husband is as well as can be expected. But he is still under a physician's care. So perhaps it would be best if…'

'No! No, it wouldn't be best—I want to see him now!'

Becca actually flinched at the sound of her own voice. It was too high, too sharp, too tight—too *everything*—and she didn't need the change that moved across the young man's face, tightening every muscle, pressing his lips together, to tell her that she had overstepped some invisible mark, one she hadn't been fully aware of. She didn't have the right, the position, in this household, to make demands like that. She had no idea what orders Andreas had given before his accident or even after it. She didn't even know whether he had given this Leander permission to contact her or if the young man had done it on his own initiative. And if that was the case…

'Please…' she added, unable to erase the raw note of desperation from her tone. 'Can I see my husband now?'

She saw doubt in the face before her and was about to give in to the despair that swamped her. But then, just as she was debating whether to open her mouth and plead or simply to try to push past him and head into the house—she could remember much of the layout of the place from the brief time she had spent in it in the past—Leander obviously reconsidered.

'Very well—if you will come this way.'

He would never know, Becca reflected, just how difficult she found it to keep behind him as he made his way up the wide, curving staircase and along the landing. With anxiety chewing at her thoughts, she wanted to rush ahead to get to Andreas' room before he did. It was only when Leander came to a halt outside an unexpected door that she was thankful that she hadn't. Because Andreas had obviously decided not to stay in the room that had been his when she had been at the villa before. The room that would have been *theirs* if the marriage hadn't broken up as soon as it had begun. And as her footsteps slowed and stopped she knew that she should be grateful.

How could she ever have gone into *that* room, with all the memories it held? How could she have coped with the past being thrown right into her face as soon as the door opened, and she saw the bed on which Andreas had made her his?

Made her his and then rejected her without a second thought.

It would destroy her, she knew. Already the way that her heart was beating high up in her throat was choking off the air to her lungs and making her head swim so that she felt faint.

So she could only be grateful when Leander opened the door to a room she had never been into and stood there waiting for her to come past him.

Becca's legs felt weak beneath her, shaking in apprehension as she forced herself to walk into the room. What would Andreas look like? What sort of a mood would he be in? He had been asking for her, yes—but *why*?

The image of her husband's dark, furious face, the black eyes blazing, the beautiful, sensual mouth drawn into a hard, slashing line floated in her mind so that for a few moments that was all she saw when she was actually standing in the room. It obscured her vision, covering the reality of the man in the bed.

But then she blinked and saw Andreas for the first time since he had slammed the door in her face almost twelve months before.

The bruises were the first things she noticed. Bruises that marred the smooth, olive-toned skin, turning it black and blue in a way that had her drawing in her breath in a sharp hiss. His eyes were closed, lush black lashes lying in dark crescents above the high cheek-bones, and a day or more's growth of beard darkened the strong line of his jaw.

Shock at the sight of him lying there so still and silent made her gasp. Her vision that had cleared for just a brief moment blurred again as tears of horror filled her eyes.

'He's unconscious!'

She didn't care that her distress showed in her voice, that the edge of fear sharpened it.

'Asleep,' Leander reassured her. 'He was unconscious for a time, but the doctors wouldn't let him out of hospital until they were sure he was on the mend.'

'Can I stay—with him?'

She didn't know what she might do if Leander refused permission. She didn't think that her legs would support her if she tried to walk out of the room. She could still barely see, and the fight to force back the tears, refusing to let them spill out down her cheeks, was one that took all her concentration.

'*Kyrie* Petrakos asked for me,' she added hastily when she saw that the younger man was hesitating. 'I promise I won't wake him—or do anything to disturb him.'

At last he nodded.

'He did ask for you,' he said, indicating a chair with a wave of his hand. 'But I should warn you that the blow to the head has left him with some memory problems—the doctors believe they will be only temporary. So he may be a little confused when he wakes. Would you like a drink sent up?'

'I'll be fine,' Becca assured him hastily, squashing down the weak thought that a cup of tea might warm the sudden coldness of her blood, give her a strength she so much needed. What she needed more was to be left alone, to have time to catch her breath, mentally, since the telephone call had rocked the balance of her world so desperately.

As Leander left the room she sank down thankfully into the chair he had indicated, her legs giving way beneath the weariness that was both mental and physical, her eyes fixed on the still form of the man in the bed.

She had promised not to wake him, not to disturb him, but

the truth was that he was disturbing her for all he lay so silent and unmoving. The sight of Andreas, whom she had last seen so tall, strong and proud, lying still and pale in the bed was almost more than she could take.

But it was worse than that.

She'd spent the last year telling herself that this man had been a mistake, one she deeply regretted, but she was over him. It had taken just one glance at the man in the bed, at the dark, stunning profile, the broad naked chest where the bronzed skin showed livid, disturbing bruises, ones that made her heart clench just to see them, to rock that belief in her head. If she had seen him standing, if her first awareness had been of the powerful, forceful man he was, the man who had used her and then thrown her out of his home, perhaps it would have been different. This man was too quiet, too vulnerable.

Too deceptively vulnerable, a warning voice sounded inside her head. Because at any other time, vulnerable was not a word she would ever associate with Andreas Gregorie Petrakos.

'I hate him.'

In a low, desperate whisper, she tried the word hate out for size, feeling it strange and alien on her tongue. For almost a year now, she had used it every day in connection with Andreas' name. Used it and meant it.

'I hate Andreas Petrakos,' had been the first words she had said on waking and often the last ones that had been on her tongue at night. They had replaced and reversed the ones that had been there before, in the brief time before her marriage, when she had whispered to herself how much she loved this man, afraid to voice the thoughts aloud for fear that she might be tempting fate and the happiness she dreamed of would evaporate just as a result of saying them.

She shouldn't have bothered, Becca told herself bitterly.

She hadn't tempted fate but the cruel blow had fallen after all. Andreas had never loved her as she had loved him; in fact, his marrying her had only been an act of revenge.

The man in the bed sighed, stirred, muttered something, immediately drawing her eyes to his face once again. Had those heavy, closed eyelids flickered once or twice, or was she just deceiving herself?

Just the thought of it made her heartbeat kick up several notches, making her blood pound in her ears.

What would she do if—when he woke? When he spoke?

And what about these 'memory problems'? How much had they affected him? Knowing Andreas as she did, she could just imagine how difficult he would find any limitation to his awesome mental abilities. He would hate it and it would chafe at him like a net thrown over a wounded lion, holding him captive. He would rage against it, and Andreas in a rage was a terrifying sight.

But perhaps more importantly, she should also consider what this news meant for her. Would Andreas even remember that he had asked for her? And what had been on his mind when he had?

The long-fingered hand that lay on the bed had definitely twitched, flexing briefly as he sighed again. There was a long, angry-looking scratch running from the base of his ring finger right to his wrist and it pulled on something deep in her heart to see the raw tear in the beautiful, bronzed skin that seemed so very dark in contrast to the soft white cotton of the coverings.

Becca bit down hard on her lower lip to hold back the faint gasp that almost escaped her and she fought to push away memories of how it had felt to know the touch of that hand, have it caress her skin, rouse her to heated longing…

'No!'

She wasn't going to let herself go down that road. To do

so would destroy her even before she'd spoken to Andreas, or found out just why he'd asked for her. And she was having enough trouble holding on to her self-control as it was, with the bitter memories that assailed her at just being in this house.

The *bittersweet* memories—because some of them she could never deny had been so very sweet. She had been so idyllically happy when she had arrived at the villa. So happy that she had thought that her heart would burst from sheer joy.

But that had been before Andreas had taken that loving heart and ripped it into tiny pieces.

'*O opoios…*'

There was no mistaking it this time. Andreas had murmured the words, rough and low, but he had spoken. His eyes remained closed but his head stirred restlessly against the pillows as he swallowed, ran his tongue over his dry lips.

'*O opoios…*?' he said again, his voice grating as if he hadn't used it for a long time.

'Andre…'

Becca's voice matched his for hoarseness and lack of strength. She felt as if all the blood had drained from her body at the sound of that once so dearly loved voice that she hadn't heard for a year.

'Mr Petrakos…'

That brought his eyes open in a rush, huge and dark, turning her way, frowning as he tried to focus on her face.

What could she see in them? It certainly wasn't welcome— but was it anger or rejection, or…?

'Who—?'

He heaved himself up on the pillows, propped himself on one elbow as he stared into her face, and the cold glare from his deep-set black eyes warned her that she was in trouble.

'So tell me,' he said slowly and clearly in English, 'just where the hell have you been?'

# CHAPTER TWO

'So TELL me, just where the hell have you been?'

He'd spoken in English, Andreas realised, but he had no idea why. Somehow when he'd opened his mouth, the words had just come out in that language, and he hadn't even really thought about it.

So what did that mean?

Ever since he'd come round from the coma into which he'd fallen after the accident, nothing had been clear in his thoughts at all. He hadn't even been able to remember his own name or where he lived, and it had taken a couple of long, hellish weeks for anything that he was told to stick inside his battered brain.

He'd been thrown about the car quite violently, and he'd hit his head hard, they'd told him. He was lucky to be alive, so a few scrambled thoughts, some hazy memories were not unexpected. Hazy he could cope with, scrambled too. It was the blank, empty hole where most of his memory of the past year or so should be that was really disturbing him.

But the doctors had had an answer for that, too. It would come back, they had assured him. In its own time. He just needed to relax and wait.

The problem was that no one told him how long he had to wait. Or what the hell he did if it didn't come back at all. The last thing he felt was *relaxed*.

And they never told him how to handle situations like this. Like waking up in his own room with a beautiful woman sitting in a chair, watching him.

A beautiful woman he remembered from before the gap in his mind.

She was of medium height, as much as he could tell, and with a neat, slenderly curved figure in a blue and green print dress under a short white cotton jacket. Her hair was almost as dark as his own, shaped in a neat, short feathery cut that framed the heart-shaped face, emphasising the high cheek-bones and the rich curve of her soft mouth. But where the eyes that he saw in the mirror every day were black too, hers were a soft, washed-looking pale blue, the colour of the sea out in the bay on a cool, shadowy day.

'You *are* Rebecca, aren't you?' he demanded again when the woman didn't speak but simply stared at him with wide, stunned-looking eyes.

'Yes, I'm—I'm Becca... Rebecca.'

The words were English and on the soft, hesitant voice the accent seemed to fit as well. So somehow he'd been right when he had spoken to her in English.

He didn't even really know why English, only that it had felt so right.

And something to do with this woman whose face had been the first thing that he had focused on when he opened his eyes. The woman who, he had to admit, had sparked off the first moment of real, sharp, intense interest he had felt since the day he had come round after the accident to a world turned upside down. At least he was still aware of the appeal of a beautiful female face, he thought bitterly, the sharp twist of desire reminding him that, no matter what was wrong with his mind, he was still functioning as a *man* for the first time since regaining consciousness.

And the amazing thing was that he could remember *her*. So she belonged in his life from the time before his memory had been wiped away.

Becca—Rebecca Ainsworth. The woman he had met at a party in London and who had knocked him for six from the moment he had first set eyes on her.

And the woman he must still be having a passionate relationship with—*Theos*, but he hoped it was passionate!—or else why would she have turned up here like this?

'So what took you so long?'

The look of shock combined with blank astonishment on her fine features told him better than his own ears how aggressive and hostile he had sounded. That was the result of the sudden, violent tug of attraction throwing him off balance with its hint of how things had once been—in the life he could no longer remember.

'Forgive me,' he added automatically. 'I don't find it easy living with everyone knowing more about me than I do myself. It's just a relief to see a familiar face.'

But then something about the way she looked, some movement of her head, a flash of wariness in her eyes, hastily concealed, set his nerves on edge and had him clamping his jaw tight shut on the anger that almost escaped him.

Had he got things wrong? Was Becca here because of what was still between them or had Leander decided to call her as a way of getting round the doctor's unwelcome suggestion that he have a nurse? If that was the case, then the way that

Andreas' explicit instructions had been so blatantly ignored made anger well up inside him.

'We are still together, aren't we? Or are you just here as the damn nurse?'

'Am—I...?'

Becca's thoughts spun as she saw the way that Andreas' face had changed. It seemed as if in the few brief moments since he had opened his eyes and focused on her sitting there, watching him, he had swung from one extreme of mood to another with such devastating speed that she had difficulty interpreting his feelings or keeping up with each new change.

Disbelief she had been prepared for, suspicion too. After all, they had parted on such terrible terms that she couldn't imagine that he would truly be happy to see her, even though she had been told that he had asked for her. The last memory she had of him was of him standing in the doorway of his villa, this villa, watching her walk away, his face set into stony, unyielding lines, rejection stamped into every muscle in his tautly held body. She had known without even glancing back that his arms were folded tight across his broad chest, his powerful body filling the door space, blocking it, so that there was no hope of her getting back into the house if she had been foolish enough even to try.

But she hadn't tried. Even if she had wanted to, she knew she would be a fool to consider it. One glance into those cruel black eyes, seeing the hatred and the dark fury that had burned there, had been enough to keep her feet moving doggedly forward, even though tears blinded her eyes until she could hardly see the path in front of her. And even without that black fury, she had vowed that she was never going back. Never.

'I married you for sex—for that and nothing else,' he had said, and from somewhere deep in her soul she had dragged up a fierce, savage hatred for Andreas. A hatred that burned away all the love she thought she had felt for him and left it shrivelled into ashes in what remained of her heart. She had clung on to that hatred, and fuelled it by reminding herself over and over and over just what he had said, the way he hadn't believed her.

And that hatred, that fury had been enough to get her out of there and into the taxi that he had called to take her away.

It was only when the car had rounded the corner out of sight of the villa that she had let the bitter tears fall.

But it seemed from his behaviour now that Andreas remembered nothing of that. It was the only explanation she could think of for the way he was behaving.

Memory problems, Leander had said and, tense and jittery with nerves, she hadn't thought to ask for details of what had happened. Now it seemed that she might have to face the fact that to Andreas she was the woman he had known—what? A year before? Fifteen months? It couldn't be much more than that because they had married after only four months together.

But it seemed that that wedding and the dreadful events that had followed it had been wiped from his mind. He obviously recalled nothing about their break up—or the reasons for it. So how was she to cope with that—and how was she to behave now?

'Well?'

The question was snapped out curtly. She'd hesitated too long. Patience had never been a virtue that Andreas Petrakos held in high esteem and it seemed that that at least hadn't changed.

'*Has* Leander brought you in to act as the nurse they threatened me with?'

'Do you see having a nurse to look after you as a threat?' Becca hedged, unable to control the way an instinctive smile curled up the corners of her mouth.

Of course Andreas saw the idea of having a nurse to look after him as some sort of imposition—a threat. He'd hate the thought of needing to be looked after in any way at all. And his pride would make him fight against the prospect of that happening.

The look her instinctive teasing brought her stabbed like a stiletto. Not because of any anger in it, but because there was a gleam in those deep black eyes that told her he'd caught the faint shake of laughter in her words, the twitch of her mouth.

It was an expression that forced memories from the back of Becca's mind where she had tried to hide them away for so very long. Memories of a time when she had thought that she couldn't be happier; when she had believed that this stunning, devastating man had actually loved her as much as she had loved him. She had been very definitely and very bitterly disillusioned.

'I told the doctor I didn't need any nurse fussing over me.'

'But you haven't—been well.'

To her despair, her voice caught on the words, something sharp and uncomfortable twisting in her heart at the thought of the powerful, muscled body before her being bruised and torn in the car accident she had been told about. Even as she spoke, he shifted uncomfortably, and the movement revealed more bruising, this time along his ribs, and down to the lean waist.

She would feel that way about anyone who was injured, she tried to assure herself. All that it was was a natural compassion for anyone who had been hurt. There was nothing left in her heart to make it any more.

'The hospital believed I was well enough to be sent home, and I do not need any further attention!'

'Not even from someone who doesn't fuss?'

What *was* she doing? Becca's thoughts reeled as she heard what she'd actually said. She'd practically offered to take on the job of caring for him. And to her horror that was what Andreas obviously thought too.

'You're saying you'll never fuss over me?'

The beginnings of a smile tugged at the corners of his mouth, put a gleam in those deep, dark eyes. He couldn't be *flirting* with her—could he? The contrast with the memory of the way that she had last seen those black eyes, burning with an icy flame of hatred, made her shift uncomfortably in her seat.

'No...'

Too unsettled now to sit still, Becca got to her feet, wanting to move restlessly about the room, then suddenly thinking better of her actions and returning to perch awkwardly on the arm of the chair.

'I...I'm not saying that.'

'Then what are you saying?'

Andreas' tone had sharpened as his eyes followed her uneasy movements.

'I'm not...'

The words shrivelled into nothing, drying her mouth so that she had to slick a nervous tongue over her parched lips as she tried to find some sort of answer to give him.

She didn't know this Andreas—or, rather, she had known him once but so briefly and so unbelievably that she had to struggle to remember it.

He hadn't flirted with her when they had first met. Then he had been focused, determined, his devastating personal power concentrated totally on her, so strongly that she had found it almost impossible to breathe.

Certainly, it just hadn't seemed possible that this stunning man, this multi-multimillionaire with everything in the world that he wanted—a hundred times over—and every woman in the world prepared to fall at his feet could possibly want anything to do with plain, simple, unimpressive Rebecca Ainsworth.

And it seemed that Rebecca Ainsworth was whom he remembered. Not the fact that she had ever become Rebecca Petrakos. She didn't know what she could tell him about what had happened in the time he couldn't recall, but there had to be something. If she announced now, starkly and matter-of-factly that she was his wife—his alienated wife, the wife he had thrown out of his home with the furious order never, ever even to think of coming back there—did she even know if he would believe her?

She remembered once being told how an amnesia victim 'forgot' the time they didn't *want* to remember. That the condition could be as much psychological as it was physical. And if that was the case, had Andreas forgotten her because he couldn't bear to remember that they had been married? Some time soon, inevitably, he must get his memory back properly. And then he would know only too well just who she was.

Her heart lurched painfully at the thought. But still she wasn't brave enough to give him the truth and risk her instant dismissal.

'Andreas, you know I'm not one to fuss unnecessarily,' was all she could manage uncomfortably.

'Then I'm glad you're here to save me from someone who might.'

Andreas' tone said that that was the end of the matter, no chance of discussion, and she was still wondering just how she could take this any further when he shifted in the bed, pulling himself up even more against the pillows.

'Come here.'

It was pure Andreas; pure command. If he had snapped his fingers he couldn't have made it any more autocratic. In spite of herself, Becca pushed herself up from the arm of the chair, turning towards him, then hesitated when she saw the way that the powerful hands had closed over the bed coverings, about to throw them back.

'What are you doing?'

Her voice went up at the end of the sentence, revealing her shock and unease. When they had been together Andreas had always slept naked and the thought that he might reveal more of his powerful body than he was doing already made her blood run hot and then cold as if she was in the grip of some dangerous fever.

'I have to get up.'

The black eyes that met her shocked blue ones were wide and steady. No trace of anything other than straightforward openness lurked in their depths and his mouth showed no hint of quirking into any sort of a smile. Any double meanings or ulterior motives were in her own mind, her uncomfortable conscience making her edgy.

'And as I'm not yet as steady on my feet as I'd like to be, it might be advisable if my nurse—you—was close at hand in case of any problems.'

At least he was wearing pyjama trousers, Becca realised on a shudder of relief as the way that Andreas flung back the coverings revealed his long legs covered in navy-blue cotton. But with his chest and arms bare, there was still far too much of the beautiful olive-toned skin on display for her personal comfort.

Before the accident, he must have been working out more than ever because every inch of his upper torso was taut and toned, the muscles sharply defined, and there wasn't an ounce of spare flesh on the powerful ribcage, the narrow waist. The soft hazing of jet-black hair reminded

her painfully of the way that she had loved to smooth her
fingertips over its softness, feeling the contrast between it
and the satin skin beneath.

Should she offer a hand to help him? Her pulse jerked at
the thought of his fingers closing over hers, her throat drying
painfully so that she had to swallow hard to relieve it. After
all these months apart from him, she had managed to convince
herself that her response to Andreas' hardcore male sexuality
had been a form of mental aberration, a brief spell of madness
that had taken her over, driving her out of her sane mind and
into a world in which her normal, controlled responses no
longer ruled her actions.

But now all she had had to do was to come into his presence
once again—to move closer at his arrogant command—and
suddenly it was all happening all over again. It was as if she
breathed in the intoxicating drug of seduction simply by being
in the same atmosphere as him, drawn to him irresistibly, her
senses drugged into instant submission. And coming close to
him only made it so much worse. She could catch the inti-
mately personal scent of his skin, see the way that the sunlight
glinted on his silky black hair as he moved his head…

'Here…'

Her voice was gruff and ungracious, made that way by the
discomfort of her thoughts as she held out an arm to offer him
support. Just at the last minute she suddenly had a loss of
nerve that had her angling it so that her forearm, covered in
the white cotton of her jacket, came closest to him rather than
the bare skin of her hand.

'Thank you…I think.'

Andreas' tone of voice, the slightly cynical twist to his beautiful mouth, told her that he had noticed her hesitation, and the
careful adjustment, and misinterpreted her reasons for it.

'You were not joking when you said that you don't intend to fuss.'

'I'm sorry—I...'

Whatever she had been about to say vanished from her mind as she felt him take hold of the support she offered, strong fingers closing around her upper arm, the heat of his palm searing her skin through the soft cotton. It was as if he had attached a live electrical lead to her skin and the resulting current had raced along every nerve, fusing her thoughts. And when he put his weight onto his grip and got to his feet she was lost completely.

'Andreas...'

His name left her lips in an involuntary gasp as a response burned its way up to her brain and flashed heated memories that she had tried to erase onto a screen in her mind. From nowhere came images of the way that he had touched her before, the effect that the feel of his hand on hers had created—the things that it had led to. Her skin tingled in response to those imagined caresses, her mouth dried in wanting, longing for the feel of his lips on hers, and a rush of liquid heat flooded into her innermost core.

Without being aware of it she swayed towards him in a moment of desperate weakness, only catching herself as the movement brought her so close to the lean, powerful body that she could catch the scent of his skin, still warm from the bed, inhale the clean, masculine essence of him and feel it burn all the way down her senses. The hyper-efficient air-conditioning in the room became less than useless as a fire of response raged through her body.

The truth was that a tiny part of her wanted him to realise who she was—wanted to have the real facts out in the open and done with. But at the same time she was terrified of the repercussions of that, personally and healthwise. Until she knew just what had been said about this memory loss that Andreas was suffering from, whether it was temporary or permanent, and what the doctors had recommended, she didn't dare take any risks. And on a personal level, as soon as he realised who she was then how would he react? Would he even let her stay or would he throw her out of the house as he had done barely a year ago, with the words, 'If I never see you again it will still be too soon,' echoing in her ears?

'Becca...'

Andreas' tongue seemed to curl around the syllables, turning them into a very different sound from the one she was used to. Hot tears burned at the backs of her eyes, threatening her hard-won composure with the memory of hearing him say her name in that special way as she had lain in his arms, her head pillowed on the broad expanse of his chest, hearing the heavy thud of his heart slow gradually from the hectic pace created by the fierce passion of their lovemaking.

She didn't know if her own heart was jolting in sensual response to her memories, his touch or panic-stricken fear of the possible repercussions if—when—he realised how their relationship had changed from the one he believed it was.

'Becca...' he said again and her shocked senses, dangerously alert to everything about him, caught the change in tone, the slight thickening of his accent on her name, the faint roughness of his voice that told her without words that his mood had changed.

Curiosity had given way to interest, annoyance blending into awareness so swiftly that only someone who knew him well would notice.

But Becca knew this side of the man too well. It was the

Andreas she knew more than any other. The sexually driven man who had taught her all she knew about passion, about desire—and most of all about pleasure. She knew that when his eyes darkened so much that they seemed all black, when his voice rasped in his throat in just that way, that he was turned on, hotly aroused by what he saw.

And she had enough experience of seeing this response to know when it was directed at her.

'An—Andreas…' she tried, her voice shaking and sounding almost as rough as his.

He shook his head, slowly, silently, his eyes dropping down to watch her mouth as she spoke.

And she knew that look too. Knew the way his own mouth had opened very slightly, the slow, heavily indrawn breath. He wanted to kiss her. Wanted it so much that it absorbed all his thoughts, took all his concentration.

He wanted to kiss her and she wanted him to do just that.

Her whole body was one stinging burn of awareness from the toes that curled inside her soft leather sandals to the prickling lift of each tiny hair on her scalp. She barely felt the point at which his hand was clamped around her arm, the warmth of his palm lost in the rush of heat that scoured her skin, stripping away one much-needed protective layer and leaving her raw and yearning beneath.

But who would he be kissing? The woman he had once asked to be his wife, then flung his wedding vows in her face as he rejected her and forced her out of his house before they had even been married for twenty-four hours? The woman he couldn't remember. Or would he kiss the girlfriend—the mistress—he believed she was? The woman he didn't remember ever asking to marry him.

And if he did kiss her would the moment that their lips

touched jolt something in his brain, loosening whatever blockage kept him from recalling her?

She would risk it, she knew. From the moment that he had touched her, she had been lost. Adrift on the heated sea of physical hunger that he had always been able to wake in her.

She wanted him to kiss her. Wanted it so much that it was like a thundering, pounding refrain inside her head, so heavy and loud that she felt sure he must either hear it declared out loud, or read it burning behind the eyes she couldn't find the strength to drag away from his stunning face.

*Kiss me.*

She could almost believe that she'd said the words herself, they sounded so loud and clear in her thoughts.

*Please kiss me.*

Andreas drew in a breath, heavy and low, then let it out again in a sigh. His head was angled slightly to one side, his gleaming black eyes hooded under heavy lids, the lush, thick lashes brushing his cheeks for a moment as he looked down, taking in her upturned face in a single, sweeping glance.

'Beautiful…' he murmured, his voice even huskier than before.

'I…'

Becca tried to speak and failed, ending up with her mouth slightly open simply because she couldn't make herself close it. She felt as if she was surrounded by Andreas, by the warmth of his body, the scent of his skin. Just inches away from her she could see the way his powerful chest rose and fell with each breath he took, almost hear the beat of his heart underneath the smooth, olive-toned flesh. It was as if the world had ceased to exist. As if there was only the two of them and the heated, sensual bubble they had created around them.

With that black-eyed gaze holding her still, frozen hypno-

tised, he lifted his hand and touched the backs of his fingers
to her skin at her temple and then trailed them slowly down
her cheek, tracing the line of her jaw, her chin. When the
strong fingers reached her still open mouth, moving over the
outline of her lips, it was all that Becca could do to hold back
a moan of response. The temptation to part her lips even
more, to let her tongue slide out and curl over that stroking
fingertip, to feel the slightly salty tang of it on her tongue,
remember how it had been to taste him all over, anywhere—
everywhere—was almost irresistible.

But just as she drew in her breath, taking some of the
essence of him in with it, fighting the primitive, carnal hunger
that had suddenly reached out to enclose her, she hesitated for
a second, for the space of a single heartbeat, suddenly terrified, painfully, cruelly aware of how far from wise such an
action was.

And the next moment she could only be grateful for that
sudden flash of control, of self-preservation. Because unexpectedly that stroking hand slowed, stilled, and then was
abruptly snatched away, the rush of cold air where its warmth
had once been and the sense of loss cruel enough to force her
to bite down hard on her lower lip to hold back the cry of
shock that almost escaped her.

'I think not,' Andreas said sharply, the tone of his voice
putting distance between them more effectively than the
single step he took, backwards and away from her. 'This is
not a good idea.'

While she was still recovering from a rejection that had had
as much emotional force to her as a cruel slap in the face, he
turned on his heel and strode away from her, flinging open a door
in the opposite wall that obviously led to an *en suite* bathroom.

'I need a shower—I'll come down when I'm ready. Get

Leander to show you to a room. We'll talk about how we handle this later.'

Just like that, she was dismissed and he strode into the bathroom, the door slamming behind him. A moment later she heard the key turning firmly in the lock as if he felt the need to make very sure it was secure against...

Against what? Did he think that she might actually try to go in there after him? That she was weak enough, foolish enough—*desperate* enough to try to follow him to fling herself into his arms?

Just what had she shown in her face when he had touched her? How much of herself, of her innermost thoughts had she given away? Knowing that he didn't remember the truth about their relationship, had she been stupid enough to let her expression reveal the pain it had brought her in the time he couldn't recall?

Or perhaps his sudden reaction just now was because he was *beginning* to remember?

Becca found that she was trembling all over, her legs shaking beneath her so that she didn't feel they could support her any longer. Weak and unable to keep herself upright, she sank down onto the bed, covering her face with her hands. But her respite was brief because almost immediately she jumped up again, unable to bear the way the sheets were still warm from his body, still imprinted with the scent of his skin.

She could still feel him all around her, enveloping her in warmth. In her memory she could taste his kisses on her lips as strongly as if he had actually kissed her just now and not just dismissed her without a second's thought. But in her mouth the sense of rejection was bitter, reminding her cruelly of how she had once felt when he had denounced and banished her from his life on the black day that had been their wedding day.

*If I never see you again it will be too soon.*

The words rang inside her head, reminding her of the pain and disillusionment she had felt at that time. The same hurt and bitterness that she was risking feeling all over again just by being here.

'Oh, Becca, Becca, you *idiot*!' she reproved herself harshly as she moved as far away from the bed as she could.

She had trapped herself well and truly and the only way to get out of this was to admit to Andreas just what had happened…

'Oh, no…'

The words escaped from her lips in a whisper at the thought of confronting the cold, heartless anger she knew her husband to be capable of if she told him the truth. And besides, hadn't she read somewhere that it was foolish, even dangerous to tell someone suffering from amnesia the truth about their situation? It was forbidden, wasn't it? And she certainly wasn't about to take the risk of confronting Andreas with something he couldn't possibly want to know.

But he *had* asked for her.

That was what Leander had said, wasn't it?

Wasn't it?

The truth was that she was so emotionally battered by everything that had happened in the last few weeks that single events were beginning to blur into one big, confused and confusing mass. She had barely recovered from the curt, totally businesslike reply Andreas had sent to her first enquiry before the phone call about the accident had come through, and as soon as she had heard that she had been on the plane out to Greece, to this tiny island that Andreas called home—and that once she had hoped, dreamed would be her home too.

She couldn't remember too clearly the actual words that had

been used. But there was no way she would be here now if
Andreas hadn't actually given his permission for her to be here.

But had that been before or after he had lost his memory?
And was it the lover he believed she still was that he had asked
for—or the wife he had rejected so completely?

Behind the door of the bathroom, the noise of the shower
running jolted her back to the present, dragging her thoughts
in the last possible direction that she wanted them to go. It
was impossible to hear the driving sound of the water and not
think of the times when she had had the freedom to join him
in the shower, to share the hot water as it pounded down onto
Andreas' hard, lean body, cascading over the bronzed skin,
flowing down from the broad, straight shoulders, past his
narrow waist, over the tight curves of his…

'No!'

Becca shook her head sharply as the word escaped her, just
the image of what she was remembering enough to drive her into
motion, pushing her towards the door as fast as she could go.

'I can't take this—can't do it…'

She would find Leander, explain that there had been a
mistake. A terrible mistake.

And then she would get out of here.

She would run from Andreas as she had run a year before.
Putting as much distance between him and herself as she
possibly could.

She would run and run and she would never come back.

She should never have come back. Never, ever have come
back to the island, to the villa—to the man she had once loved
so deeply and so desperately.

What could have possessed her to even think that she could
talk to him, persuade him to listen to her, to help her…?

She was almost at the top of the stairs when the word

'help' sounded in her thoughts again, stopping her dead, reminding her of the real reason why she was here. The reason she had forgotten.

Oh, how could she have forgotten Macy? And most of all, how could she have forgotten little Daisy?

Daisy was just a baby—and her life, her tiny, precious life, depended on the way that Becca acted now.

Without her help, Daisy would die. And Becca had promised that she would do anything she could—everything she could—to help.

Standing with her hand on the newel post, fingers clenching tight over the polished wood, Becca sighed, half turned, looked back at the still slightly open door into the bedroom from which she had just fled in a panic-stricken rush.

She had promised—and she would keep that promise, no matter what it took. She needed Andreas' help and she would have to get that help, whatever she had to do to get it. She had no choice.

If the only way she could stay in the villa, the only way she could get close to Andreas and stay there until at last he remembered who she was and what she had asked of him—the money he had promised to provide—was to pretend to be the mistress that he believed her to be, then she was going to have to do it. She would play the part to the best of her ability and pray that it wouldn't take too long for Andreas' memory to return.

She had to—for Daisy's sake.

Drawing in a long, ragged breath and letting it out again on a heartfelt sigh, she made herself place first one foot on the staircase and then another, straightening her shoulders, holding her chin up high as she headed downstairs.

# CHAPTER THREE

ANDREAS turned up the power and the temperature on the shower so that it pounded down savagely onto the top of his head, thudding onto his skull, leaving him incapable of thinking.

At least that was the plan. But somehow, when he needed it most, the plan didn't seem to be working.

He wanted to forget about the moments out in his bedroom when he had touched Becca.

When he had wanted to do so much more than touch. Certainly much more than fasten his hand around hers, or to stroke his fingers along the peachy softness of her cheek.

He had wanted to kiss her so badly. The hunger to take her lips with his had been like a nagging ache throughout his whole body, adding further discomfort to the already painful bruises that made his muscles throb, tugged at his ribs when he drew in his breath sharply. He wanted to hold her, caress her. He had felt his heart kick up, his blood pulse through his veins.

He had felt himself come alive for the first time in days.

In the days that he could remember anyway. The days that had registered in the void that had been his mind since he had come round from the unconsciousness that that car crash had put him into.

And for the first time since the accident he had felt like a man again, passionate and burning with a hot, hungry desire.

But a desire he really shouldn't give in to.

'Hell and damnation!'

Andreas swore viciously and reached up to change the temperature of the water yet again, shuddering as this time an icy blast thundered onto his soaked hair, his bare shoulders. A long cold shower was what he needed to cool the heat in his blood, the fire that threatened to destroy his ability to think at all.

Any desire he felt would be crazy, stupid—madness to act upon, no matter how strongly he felt it, how urgently it called to him to appease it. He didn't need any further complications in his life. Things were already complex enough.

Wasn't it bad enough that he couldn't remember anything about the past twelve months? That anything he had learned about that year, and his accident, was something that he had had to take on trust, both in the hospital and since arriving home?

Home.

This time Andreas snapped off the shower completely and stepped out of the glass-walled stall, shaking his head like a big, angry dog, trying to drive away another flurry of unwanted thoughts that assailed and tormented him.

'Home!'

He flung the word like a curse at his reflection in the huge, steamed-up mirror, scowling blackly into the dark blur of his eyes as he did so.

This *was* his home; he knew that at least. But from the moment that he'd arrived at the door, he had had the appalling feeling that something was very wrong. And that feeling had stayed with him as he'd walked through the house.

What he'd not been prepared for was the sheer wave of desolation that had overwhelmed him at just the thought of going into the obvious room, the master bedroom. There was no way he'd been prepared to admit to it, so he had turned instead and headed for the bedroom that was furthest away from it.

Which was why he had ended up in here.

Shaking his head again, he snatched up a towel and began to dry himself, his movements rough and almost aggressive as if he could wipe away the frustration of his lack of memory along with the water drops.

'Damn!'

An unthinking movement caught the towel on a particularly dark-coloured bruise, making him draw in his breath in a sharp hiss between his teeth. But the stab of pain was easily dismissed, pushed out of his mind. It would heal. Another week or so and he would be back to normal. In his body at least.

But what about his mind?

Another string of curses, darker and even more vicious, spilled from his lips as he considered the prospect.

Without a memory or any knowledge of what had happened in the past year, how could he even think of any sort of relationship with a woman, even just the physical one that his hungry senses had been urging him on to? How could he ever allow himself any sort of emotional life when he knew nothing about the past one? He'd recognised Becca—remembered how he had felt about her. But what stage was that relationship at now?

That was certainly not a question he was ever going to ask Leander. There were some things that were too personal even for a personal assistant.

Flinging the wet towel away and snatching up a black towelling robe, Andreas shrugged it on and belted it tightly around himself, ignoring yet another protest from his bruised ribs.

He couldn't stay in here a moment longer. He twisted the key savagely to unlock the door, his fingers closing tightly over the handle until the knuckles showed white.

Becca was too much temptation for him to be able to face the thought of her staying in the house when he wasn't able to act on the sensual provocation she offered simply by existing. Just the memory of the way that his blood had heated in his veins as he'd touched her cheek had enough sting to make him fling open the door with unnecessary force.

'This isn't going to work…'

The words died on his lips as he took in the empty room, the door out onto the landing standing slightly open, showing which way she had gone.

So at least she'd done as she was told. He had been so sure that she would ignore his instructions and that when he opened the door he would find her still there, waiting for him, possibly even determined to tuck him up in bed again…

'I'm—not one to fuss unnecessarily…'

The memory of Becca's voice, soft and unexpectedly husky, speaking the words cut through another flare of sensual heat that surged along his nerves at the thought of being tucked up in bed by the lovely brunette, feeling her cool, soft hand on his brow, her fingers at his wrist checking his pulse. Immediately his pulse throbbed, desire giving him a hard, cruel kick low down in his body.

If it was this bad now, then how would it be if she stayed? What sort of 'rest and recovery' as ordered by the doctors would be possible with images such as that blazing inside his head? How could he live every day with her when just the sight of her woke a carnal hunger that he could barely restrain?

And how could he give in to that hunger when he didn't know

a thing about the missing months they must have spent together? It was better if she left, at least until he recovered somewhat.

His mind made up, he strode to the wardrobe, began pulling out clothes—a shirt and jeans—taking underwear from a drawer. He pulled on his clothes, and then headed down the stairs, bare feet padding silently on the polished wooden steps. The afternoon was coming to an end, the fierce heat of the day easing a little.

It was the sound of her laughter that caught him first. A light, bubbling sound, it seemed to reach out into the atmosphere and curl around his senses, soft and low. Just for a moment his footsteps slowed, bringing him to a halt a couple of stairs from the bottom as he paused, allowing himself to reconsider.

So what was wrong with a little flirtation—a sensual distraction from reality? They were both adults and she was as attracted to him as he was to her. She hadn't pulled away from his touch, in fact she had wanted more from him. He had seen it in her eyes. In the way that that luscious pink mouth had parted on a faint gasp. So what if he couldn't offer her a future? He didn't think she'd care about that. She'd obviously stayed around for the past year, so she must be happy with what they had.

Her laughter came again, but this time something in the sound grated on him. It sounded different, changed. Was that a flirtatious note that had slid into it?

From nowhere it seemed as if a cloud had invaded his mind. His mood changed, shifted, darkened, his whole body stiffening in the aggressive reaction of a bad-tempered dog that had just seen a stranger invade his territory.

Slowly, silently, he took a single step downwards towards the hall.

From this position he could see into the room, see where Becca was sitting at the table, a glass of some clear liquid in her hand. She was leaning back in her chair, looking so very much more relaxed than at any moment in his room upstairs. Her dark hair fell in seductive disarray around her beautiful, animated face. She'd taken off her lightweight jacket too and it hung, half on and half off the back of the chair, one sleeve dangling onto the floor. She was looking at someone else, those stunning, sea-coloured eyes fixed on whoever it was opposite her, across the table. And she was smiling.

That smile caught on Andreas' nerves. Caught and held and twisted. He found himself torn between two totally contrasting sensations. In one moment he experienced a real delight in seeing that smile, seeing the way it lit up her face, the way it curved the fullness of her lips, softening the kissable mouth and making it infinitely more tempting than before, and at the same time endured something else. That 'something else' was a feeling that was the total opposite of delight, totally at war with pleasure. Without knowing where it had come from, Andreas suddenly found that he was filled with a black fury, racked with a terrible sense of hatred that had him clenching his hands into hard fists at his sides, biting down fiercely on his bottom lip to stop himself from speaking and letting the savage anger that crouched inside him out into the open.

'I never thought of it that way,' Becca said and even her voice was very different from the way it had sounded before. It was light and easy, relaxed and touched with a hint of flirtatious teasing. 'But now that you've explained it—it makes total sense.'

'Of course it does,' a second voice put in. A deeper, thickly accented voice. A male voice and one that Andreas recognised at once.

It was Leander's voice. Leander his PA. Leander, his young, tall, dark and handsome PA.

A terrible sense of jealousy ripped through him, driving away all sense of rationality, all hope of calm. His jaw tightened, clamped into a thin, hard line until it ached and he could feel the rage rising in him like lava in a volcano, boiling up to the surface and threatening to spill out over the top, engulfing everything in a blazing, burning flood of fire.

Another slow, silent step downwards moved him to a position where he could see fully into the room. He could see where Leander lounged against the wall, long legs crossed at the ankles, dark face smiling, a glass in his own hand.

'Never argue Greek legends with a Greek,' the younger man said now, waving his drink in the air to emphasise his point, his smile seeming to Andreas' watchful gaze to be intimate, almost conspiratorial.

'I won't,' Becca said and the gleam of amusement in her face, the smile she directed at Leander twisted a knife deep inside Andreas.

He could feel his head start to pound, his breath becoming raw and uneven. He didn't ask himself where the rage was coming from, just accepted it as right, as the way he should feel. Wasn't this why he had told himself she had to go? That she was trouble if she stayed around?

He'd had enough.

Taking the last two steps down in a single jump, he marched into the room, his black mood showing in every stride, every movement. His attention totally focused on Becca, he saw the way that her head swung round, eyes widening in sudden confusion.

And guilt? Perhaps there was a touch of it. Certainly her face went white enough to make it seem that way.

'OK, that's it,' he snapped, watching her eyelids flutter, her long dark lashes dipping to conceal her gaze just for a moment in a reaction to his appearance that she couldn't disguise.

'It's time you left. Time you were out of here—*now,*' he added more forcefully when she simply sat back in her chair and stared at him, her mouth very slightly open, those beautiful eyes now blinking hard in shock as if she couldn't believe what she was hearing.

'But…'

'Andreas…' Leander put in but Andreas ignored him and addressed his words straight into Becca's stunned face.

'Did you hear what I said?'

'Oh, I heard all right…'

Becca was having to struggle to keep control of her voice enough to answer him. Her heart had lurched so hard, so violently when Andreas had come into the room that just for a moment she had thought she might actually faint from the shock of it. But even as she recovered a whole new tide of emotions had swept over her, a sense of apprehension so fierce as to be almost total panic being uppermost amongst them.

What was happening? Why was Andreas behaving like this? Earlier that afternoon, upstairs in his room, he had been distant it was true, but polite enough. Now he was in a dark, icy rage, his handsome features set into a mask of total hostility and rejection that made the panic come worryingly closer, her heart fluttering disturbingly and her thoughts whirling out of control.

Had he remembered what had happened? Had something she'd done betrayed her so that Andreas had realised the true situation between them and had now come downstairs in savage rage to turn on the wife he had rejected so brutally twelve months ago and force her out of his home once again?

'But I've only just unpacked.'

'Then pack again,' he commanded, eyes like cruel lasers fixed on her confused and worried face.

She knew this mood of old and it frightened her. When he was like this, then Andreas had no intention of yielding anything—he would not be swayed in any way. Harsh memories of the way that he had flung almost exactly those words at her a year before now resurfaced and threatened to take all her emotional strength away at a blow.

At last the haze in her mind was easing enough for her to be able to see him clearly but just the sight of him was enough to rock her composure once again.

His pure white shirt was worn casually loose, clinging to broad, straight shoulders and falling softly over the leather belt at his waist, the narrow hips. The fine cotton contrasted sharply with the hardness of taut muscle underneath, the pale colour throwing the golden tones of his skin into sharp, devastating contrast. His jeans had been worn and washed so many times that they were faded and rubbed, actually beginning to rip in places, and clinging with an almost sensuous closeness to the long, powerful legs. The hems were frayed where they fell over long, narrow feet, the toes curling slightly on the polished wooden floor. He looked much more like some untamed, unsophisticated Greek shepherd, or perhaps a fisherman, rather than the urbane and powerful multimillionaire he actually was. And, when he was dressed as simply and as casually as this, it was the sheer physical power of the man that hit home hard and strong, knocking her off balance fast with his appeal to the most primitive, most basic part of her female nature. Her blood was pulsing in her veins so much that she almost missed it when he spoke again.

'Pack up and get out.'

'But you said—'

'I know what I said and I've changed my mind. I don't need a woman in my life and certainly not one who's going to spend her time flirting with the rest of my staff.'

*Flirting...*

Well, at least there was one tiny hint of something that might give her a hope that all was not lost. Flirting, he'd said. So if a touch of jealousy was his problem, then perhaps the game was not up after all. Perhaps there was still a chance that he hadn't realised the truth about who she was.

It would be a bitter irony if he had. After the moment of weakness when she'd fled the bedroom in a panic, she had finally managed to get a grip on herself. It was the thought of Daisy that had done it. The memory of the tiny, frail little body she had last seen inside a hospital incubator, wires and tubes seeming to be attached to each tiny limb, to every inch of the baby's skin. She could still hear in her head the doctor's voice, giving them the terrible, the soul-destroying truth.

Daisy was a desperately sick little baby. To save her life she needed a vital operation—an operation that was so new, so experimental that only one surgeon in America had ever performed it successfully. If they could find the money...

Becca shuddered inwardly as she recalled the overwhelming despair that she and Macy had suffered at that moment. There was no way...no way but one.

Daisy's plight was what had brought her to speak to Andreas in the first place. Surely, even hating her as he did, her ex-husband could not harden his heart against the tiny girl. If only she could stay here long enough for him to regain his memory so that she could ask him for help. That image had stiffened her spine and brought her downstairs fired by a new determination to succeed. It had even given her the courage to tell Leander a version of the truth. That Andreas had been asking for her and so she was here to take care of him.

To her delight and amazement Leander had not only supported her idea, he had even got straight on the phone to the agency to tell them the nurse they had been asked to provide would not be needed.

'After all,' Leander had said, 'who better to care for a man than his wife?'

Leander, Becca decided, had a strong sentimental streak in him. But, as he had never met her when she had been in his employer's life, then he obviously didn't know that sentimental was the last way that Andreas would feel about his particular wife. But she didn't disillusion him. Having Leander on her side was more than she could hope for, and just that one small gesture of support had made her feel that she could stay. That she might just be able to handle this—and hope to save baby Daisy as a result. She had even started to relax just a little.

But that had been before Andreas had appeared in the room, stiff-necked and scowling, with dark fire in his eyes, and ordered her to pack up and go, destroying all her hopes in a single moment.

'I wasn't flirting.'

Somehow she imposed the control she needed over her voice and made it sound calm and just a trifle indignant. She had to keep the pain of the last eleven months out of her voice. That would give her away for sure.

But Andreas' current lover—the mistress he assumed her to be—would feel much more able to cope with his temper and his jealousy.

'No?'

The mocking lift of one black eyebrow questioned her response in a way that almost shook her confidence. But she couldn't let him get to her. For Daisy's sake she had to be strong—for Daisy's sake she had to make sure that she stayed here.

'No!'

The forceful emphasis got his attention, making those deep-set eyes widen just for a moment before his handsome features settled back into their expression of cynical scepticism.

'Can I point out that you were the one who told me to come downstairs…?'

The affronted tone was a good idea. It was quite clear that he hadn't expected her indignation and was decidedly taken aback by it.

'The one who lo…'

No, don't mention the locked door or protest about it—that would take things to a deeper level. One that was clouded by the past between them that he remembered nothing about.

'The one who told me not to fuss.'

That actually won her a tiny sign of acknowledgement from the dark, distant man before her. Not a nod, that would have been too much of a concession, but the proud head inclined faintly to one side and something flickered in the black eyes that might have been respect.

'*Kyrie* Petrakos…'

It was Leander who spoke, inserting his words carefully into the tensely silent stand-off that had come between them. He said something in Greek, speaking swiftly and, Becca thought, rather nervously. Obviously Leander felt that his job was on the line—so would he continue to support her?

Andreas' response was in the same language, sharp and obviously dismissive—a dismissal that was repeated when the younger man hesitated, looking distinctly uncomfortable and unsure.

'It's all right, Leander,' Becca put in, turning to him, wanting to reassure him. 'You don't have to worry about me.'

Out of the corner of her eye she could sense Andreas' head snap round, feel the dark fire of his eyes burning into the back of her head as she spoke, and she could see the reflection of the furious glare in the concern on Leander's face. But she made herself smile, pretending at a composure she was far from feeling.

'Really...' she said. 'This isn't your problem.'

As she watched Leander leave, the silence behind her seemed to grow all the more ominous, all the more oppressive, and she held her breath as the door swung to after him, waiting for the inevitable explosion that she had sparked off with her response.

# CHAPTER FOUR

TO HER astonishment it didn't come. Instead there was a faint, soft sound. The sound of Andreas drawing in his breath and letting it out again in a deliberate attempt at control.

'So who put you in charge?' he drawled cynically. 'Who gave you permission to give my staff orders?'

'Not orders.'

Becca caught her own breath, aiming to match his cold-toned restraint as she made herself turn round, coming to face him. She wouldn't let his imposing stature, the arrogant set of his jaw, or the cold light in his eyes overawe her. If she did then he would win and she knew that Andreas Petrakos had never lost this sort of a battle in his life. He hadn't almost tripled the family fortune in his thirty-three years by being anyone's pushover, least of all any woman's. But she had to manage this somehow; had to win herself at least permission to stay. The repercussions for Daisy if she didn't were too terrible even to consider. She wasn't going to let herself even imagine the possibility of defeat.

'You'd already told him to leave. I was just making sure that he didn't feel obliged to stay to protect me.'

'You understand Greek?'

Just for a moment Andreas sounded so taken aback that Becca actually allowed herself the smallest hint of a smile. Typical male—typical *Greek* male, she told herself. He made assumptions from his lordly position in charge of everything and was stunned to find that perhaps those suppositions and his assessment of the situation were not quite as perfect as he believed.

'I don't have to know precisely what words you used to know just what you meant,' she pointed out. 'So tell me, do you always order everyone around as if they were a dog that was yours to command?'

'Leander values his job too much to do anything stupid.'

'Leander knows that you're in a vicious mood and liable to bite his head off if he didn't do as he was told. You surely didn't really think that I was flirting with him? You have to know that...'

Yikes, no!

Mentally Becca screeched to a halt, slamming the brakes on the foolishly betraying words she had almost let slip. Don't go down that road—just don't!

Had she really been about to say to Andreas's face that he had to know that when he was in a room—anywhere nearby—any other man just didn't have a chance? That beside his incandescent male sexuality, every other male within a hundred miles became just a shadow of himself, fading into insignificance beside Andreas?

'I have to know that what?' Andreas enquired with silky menace when she caught herself up, biting hard on her foolish tongue. His brilliant dark eyes had narrowed sharply, the look he turned on her from them shrewdly assessing, and to Becca's horror she felt a rush of embarrassed heat flooding her cheeks.

'That I'm with you,' she managed to force out.

Her voice grew stronger as she recalled her thoughts of moments before, putting them into words to get herself out of the hole she had dug for herself. If she was his current mistress, then she would probably laugh off Andreas' over-reaction just now.

'And even if you don't want anyone to fuss, if you're determined to dismiss your staff like that, then someone needs to keep an eye on you.'

'And you're happy to do that?'

'Of course.'

Did his question mean that perhaps he was reconsidering? That he would let her stay after all? Behind her back, Becca crossed her fingers secretly. She didn't know what she would do if Andreas still insisted that she leave.

'You should sit down.'

She waved a hand towards the nearest chair, cursing the way that, in her own eyes at least, her fingers' unwanted tremor gave away too much to that cold-eyed scrutiny.

'And would you like something to drink? Water? Coffee?'

'Wine?'

It was a deliberate provocation and a wicked gleam in his black eyes told her that he was testing her. But he moved towards the chair just the same.

'You're just out of hospital after a nasty accident. Do you think wine is a good idea? How about thinking of something else?'

'I would but you'd probably veto that as well,' Andreas tossed at her surprisingly lightly, but Becca noticed that he took the seat she'd indicated all the same.

He sank down into it with every appearance of ease and lounged back, stretching out his long legs and crossing them at the ankles. He looked as if he was simply relaxing but there was a slight tightness to his mouth, a shadow on his skin that reminded her he was still convalescent. Pushing back her own chair, she got hastily to her feet.

'I'll get you some water, then.'

'If that is all that you're offering…'

Andreas' reply stopped her in mid-flight to the kitchen, and she froze for a moment before she turned slowly back again. Had she heard right? Was that note in his voice what she thought it had been?

Was it possible that Andreas was actually *flirting* with her?

She realised what had happened. She had taken the route in the conversation that she would have done when they were together and an argument had broken out. She had stood up for herself, refused to give in to his anger, then she had moved the subject away and on to another topic entirely—and Andreas had followed her. Just as he had used to do when they were together, he had let himself be eased out of his bad mood and into another, very different one.

But was this different mood any less dangerous than before?

There was one thing she did know and that was that the way to make Andreas reveal his hand when he was determined to keep it hidden was to challenge him—call his bluff. And although he might not remember her or their life together, this was still Andreas, wasn't it? She had to know where she stood and she thought she knew the way to go about it.

'Water…' she said firmly, hoping she sounded more confident than she actually was as she headed into the kitchen.

He didn't need a drink—well, definitely not water, Andreas reflected as Becca marched into the kitchen, hunted around and found some bottled water in the fridge, but if she wanted to get him water then he was quite happy to let her. Anything so that he could watch her, enjoy the sway of her hips in the delicate blue dress as she walked, the way her breasts swung gently as she bent down to look in the fridge, the neat, precise movements of those soft hands—the hands he still remembered resting on his when she'd stood beside his bed—as she twisted open the bottle of water.

The truth was that he enjoyed sitting here and watching her move around his home, letting her take care of him. He was even enjoying his body's instinctive reaction to having her around. The insistent clamour of his senses, the way he became hard just watching her might be frustrating and uncomfortable on one level, but at least he felt alive in a way that he hadn't known since the accident. She was a hell of a lot more attractive than Leander or Medora, his devoted but matronly housekeeper. Medora might be the closest thing he had ever had to a mother, but she wasn't a delight to watch like this woman.

This beautiful woman.

This beautiful, sexy woman.

This beautiful, sexy woman whom he wanted more than...

Hell and damnation, how could he say that he wanted her more than he had ever wanted her in the time they had been together, when he only remembered the smallest part of that time? The first weeks after they had met. And the most vivid memory he had of that time was of wanting this woman in his bed, just as he did now.

So was anything different in any way? He just knew that he wanted her so badly that it had made him act like a fool.

Andreas sighed and raked both his hands through his hair as he went back over the way he had behaved, the way that he had lost his temper so completely when he had seen Becca with Leander. Seen them talking together—laughing—flirting, he had believed. His anger had been like a red mist before his eyes. A burning mist that had pushed him into action without stopping to think.

But now that he'd calmed down he was going to have to apologise to his PA for snarling at him like a savagely jealous dog guarding a particularly juicy bone.

Andreas' mouth twisted wryly.

Jealous?

Was that how he felt when he was jealous? The problem was that he had nothing to compare it with. He couldn't honestly say if he had ever felt like that before. Had he ever been reduced to that sort of fury because he thought someone else had what he wanted? Had he set out to ruin a good thing because he felt so savagely angry?

Because Becca could be a good thing. He didn't need to have any past reference points to tell him that; the effect that she had on him—on his body—on his senses—in the present was quite enough.

And he didn't need telling that that was why he had been so blackly angry. Because he wanted her so damn much that it had clouded his judgement.

He'd make it right with Leander tomorrow. But he'd also make it clear that the younger man should keep his hands off. Becca was *his* and he wouldn't allow anyone else to interfere.

She was coming back towards him now, the glass in her hand, and if the back view had been good then the front was so much better. The determination in her walk drew attention to those slender, curving hips and under the soft cotton her even softer breasts moved in a way that made his mouth dry. Her head was held high, stubborn little chin tilted deliberately and the fire in her eyes made him smile to himself at the enticing prospect of the battle to come.

'Your water.'

Becca thrust the glass at him without finesse or ceremony and only the fact that his reflexes were swift and accurate stopped it from upending all over him.

'I prefer it in the glass,' he murmured drily, earning himself an expected glare of reproof that made those sea-coloured eyes flash like polished gems. The trite cliché 'You're beautiful when you're angry' hovered on his lips but he swallowed it down with a sip of the water, opting for not provoking her any further, and murmured carefully polite thanks instead.

'You're welcome,' Becca retorted in a voice that made a nonsense of the courteous reply. 'Enjoy your drink.'

It was as she swung away from him, turning on her heel with a dismissive little gesture of one hand, that he suddenly had the clear idea that he knew exactly what she was going to do. Her determined steps towards the door confirmed as much, making his lips twitch in suppressed amusement.

'Are you going somewhere?'

She spared him another of those swift, flashing glares over her shoulder.

'To my room—to pack, seeing as you've made it so plain that you don't want me here. It would have been easier if you'd told me *before* I emptied my case.'

He let her get right to the door, waiting a carefully calculated moment, watching for the almost imperceptible hesitation in the fingers that reached for the handle...closed over it...flung it open...

'You can stay,' he said quietly, stopping her dead halfway out the door.

For a second or two he thought she hadn't heard. Her foot was actually still held out in front of her, preparing to take the next step. But then, very slowly and silently, she lowered it to the ground, and stood still.

'What did you say?' she asked, not looking at him but staring straight ahead of her, into the now shadowy hallway.

'I said you can stay.'

For a moment Becca couldn't move. She felt as if she didn't know what to think—how to think. She had the strangest feeling as if time had suddenly gone backwards and she and Andreas were back in the past, in the time when they had been together, before they were married.

Her strategy had worked exactly as she had planned it would. She had called his bluff, made it appear that she was about to leave, and he had let her get so far and then called her back. He was going to let her stay.

She should feel triumphant—she should feel happy. Andreas' change of heart meant that she could have a hope of talking to him about Daisy—about the money so desperately needed to give her baby niece a chance of life. But she only knew a tiny glimmer of triumph and her other feelings were so complicated and mixed up that they kept her frozen, her eyes wide and sightless. Before she could talk to him about Daisy he would have to recover his memory and the momentary glimpse she had just had into a past where they had been together—*happy* together—tore at her heart with the reminder of how it would be when he recalled the truth. He had thrown her out of the house, out of his life, because he believed she was only after his money. The thought of his reaction when he learned that she was only here now because of money again drained the blood from her limbs, making her legs tremble beneath her.

'Becca? Did you hear what I said?'

She had hesitated too long, arousing Andreas' suspicions. Out of the corner of her eye she was aware of the fact that he had got up from his chair, looked as if he was about to come towards her.

'Yes, I heard.'

Slowly she turned back to face him, her expression carefully blank.

'You want me to stay as your nurse or as…?'

She couldn't find a word to express the alternative—lover—partner—mistress—*wife*?—and so she just let the sentence trail off unfinished.

'As whatever you want.'

Then an arrogant flick of his hand dismissed the question.

'Definitely not my nurse! You know what I think of that idea. So why don't you just stay—as my guest? Then if you think you need to keep an eye on me you can.'

'And what would I do the rest of the time?'

'Oh, I feel sure that we will think of something.'

'Like what?' Becca demanded, eyeing him warily.

A note in his voice told her that the flirtatious mood of a short time before had not, as she had thought, evaporated when she'd called his bluff by heading for the door. In fact every instinct she had ever had where this man was concerned was screaming at her that the lazy sensuality of his smile was deceptive in its indolence. The black eyes might be hooded and partially hidden under heavy lids but she could see enough of the gleam in them to know that his thoughts were not on the idea of her taking care of him—in the nursing a convalescent meaning of the words, at least.

'Like this,' Andreas murmured with misleading softness and before she was even aware of the fact that he had anything planned, or could even think of taking any avoidance moves, he took several long, firm strides forward, covering the distance between them in a matter of seconds.

This time she had no warning. This time there was no change in his voice, no hint from the look in his eyes. This time he took her completely by surprise and so instantly had the upper hand, with total control over the situation.

'Like this,' he said again, low and rough.

His hand came under her chin, holding it tight. He lifted her face towards his and his mouth came down hard on hers, taking it in a burning, searing kiss that made her thought processes stop dead, then shatter into a million tiny fragments.

She couldn't think; she could only feel. And what she felt was heat. The heat of his mouth, his breath on her skin. The heat of his arms coming round her, that long, powerful body so very close to hers. But it wasn't just a physical heat that blazed through her. There was the burning fire of response, the sensation of her blood temperature climbing higher and higher with each accelerated beat of her heart. Her whole system was going into meltdown, her mind seeming to cease to exist, her nerves, her skin, even her bones becoming molten with desire so that she sagged against him, unable to hold herself upright, and it was only the strength of his support around her that kept her from collapsing in a trembling and abandoned heap right at his feet.

'Andreas—' she began against the pressure of his lips, but the attempt to speak, to try to form some sort of protest that she was incapable of sustaining, gave him the opportunity he was waiting for.

In the moment that her mouth partly opened, Andreas seized his chance and deepened the kiss with sensual deliberation. Her parted lips were crushed even more under the passion of his, his tongue sliding into the exposed warmth, the soft moisture, tangling with hers in an intimate dance that made her senses swoon, had her fingers closing over his arms, clenching tight.

But this time it wasn't the need for support that had her

holding him close, as close as she could. This time it was pure physical need that made her clutch at him this way. The need to feel his lean, hard frame against hers, feel the pressure of the strong bones of his chest, his ribcage against her breasts, the curve of his pelvis cradling her hips. And because of that closeness there was no way she could be unaware of the swell of his forceful erection, hot and hard against her, communicating need and passion in a way that no words ever could.

Cold need and heartless passion.

The icy little voice of reason slid into her mind, stopping the heat of her reaction dead, so fast that it made her head spin.

Andreas Petrakos was totally capable of coming on full and hard with his mouth, his tongue, his body, when no part at all of his mind was involved—and least of all his *heart*!

Hadn't he shown that when he had brought her here the first time, just after their marriage? When he had brought her into the house, barely stopping to shut the door as he went through it. When he had kissed her as they mounted the stairs and taken her into the bedroom, his mouth practically welded to hers. And with his hands hotly, hungrily busy on her body, finding the fastenings of her clothing blind, dealing with them with rough haste, discarding them like a Hansel and Gretel trail leading from the hallway to his room.

And in that room he had made the hottest, most ardent, most passionate love in the world to her, waking a matching hunger in every inch of her quivering body, showing her pleasures she had never believed possible, taking her to heights of ecstasy she had never known before.

Before dropping her right down to earth again with a sickening, agonising thud, just a few, devastatingly short hours later. She still had the scars on her heart where his black cruelty had slashed into it.

And with the memory everything inside her froze in an instant. The rush of heat that had flooded her body ebbed away as fast—faster—than it had come, taking all the passion with it.

'Becca?'

Andreas had sensed her withdrawal, her stillness, and his kisses stopped, adding another terrible sensation to the thousands of whirling feelings in Becca's head and in her heart.

'No…'

It was all that she could manage and it was just a whisper. A thin thread of sound that did nothing to express what she really felt deep inside: the searing agony of loss, the desperation of knowing that she was so weak—too weak—the bitter despair of knowing that Andreas had only to touch her, to kiss her and she had fallen into his arms, into his control like a foolish child, one that had not yet learned that fire burned—again and again and again.

'No…' she tried again, managing to make it actually sound like a word this time. But she still couldn't put any real force into it. She still couldn't make it sound like the word that was ringing inside her head, screaming to be heard.

No, no, no, *no*! that voice said. Loud and clear and savagely honest. A voice that no one could doubt she meant.

But that voice was the voice of panic. The voice of pain. The voice of the woman who had once loved this man so desperately that she had rushed into marriage with him without stopping to think. It was the voice of the woman whose heart he had broken. The voice of the woman whose love had turned to hatred in the black, terrible moments as she forced herself to walk away from him—fighting a cruel bitter war with her longing to turn back, to see him just once more.

It was the voice of the woman that she couldn't let Andreas see.

Not now, not ever, at least until he had his memory back and he knew once more who she was. Not until she had had a chance to talk to him, to ask him for help for Daisy. To save the baby's life.

And even then she couldn't—wouldn't ever let him see just what he had done to her. She couldn't let him begin to guess how much he had destroyed her life.

And she most definitely couldn't do it now.

'No?'

For a moment she thought it was still her own voice screaming inside her head. But then on a jolt of her heart, she realised that it was Andreas and that he had put a darkly questioning note onto the word.

One that meant she had to find an explanation for her sudden change of mood. A reason why she had been a willing, an eager partner one moment and then slammed the brakes on hard the next. And even in her own mind, looking at her actions, she saw with a shiver how her behaviour might be interpreted. How it could seem that she didn't know her own mind or—worse—was some sort of tease who had now decided to call a sudden halt.

# CHAPTER FIVE

'You—upstairs—you said you thought this was a bad idea.'

Looking into his face, she felt her heart skip a beat as she saw the way he frowned, the black, straight brows snapping together over the brilliant eyes. Eyes that she could see were burning with frustration, with refusal to admit the need to stop. For a second she thought that he was going to argue with her but then, slowly, he nodded…

'It is a bad idea when I don't know who I am or the first thing about our past together. And you're not going to tell me about that, are you?'

That at least was easy to answer, but still Becca couldn't find any words, only managing a silent shake of her head as a reply.

'I understand. I know the doctors have said that it's better I wait for things to come back by themselves—if they come back. And that does complicate matters.'

He might be agreeing with her but he still wasn't letting her go. And somehow the fact that he wasn't actually kissing her made the way he was holding her so tight, so close, even more intimate than before.

His voice might be calm and civil, his expression controlled, but there was nothing remotely restrained or civilised in the swollen flesh that pressed so hard against her. And equally primitive was the hungry reaction that was raging through her as senses and nerves tantalised awake by the touch of Andreas' hand, the force of his kiss, were forced to adjust to the sudden loss of the heated pleasure, and protested wildly at having to do so.

'But only in that way.'

Black eyes blazed down into Becca's upturned face, the heat in them seeming to scorch her skin and making her shift uneasily from one foot to another. Andreas' intense gaze flickered for a moment as he watched the small movement, but he didn't release her or adjust his position at all. If anything he held her tighter. So tight that she could hear the heavy, powerful thud of his heart so close to her cheek, echoing her own restless pulse rate that refused to settle down into normal again.

'In every other way it felt right. So right that I don't want it to stop...'

He was drawing her close again but then, for a moment, his voice hesitated, that intent focus of his eyes seeming to blur and look clouded.

'Andr...' Becca began then let the rest of his name evaporate in a rush of sheer panic. Her heart seemed to stop, actually stand still and then lurch back into movement at a violent, uneven pace as the reason for his sudden abstraction hit home like a blow to her mind.

Was he remembering her? Starting to recall anything about his past—and about the part she had played in it?

Upstairs, in the bedroom, in the moment she had known that he wanted to kiss her and before he had run his hand down her cheek in the gesture that had torn at her heart, he had had just this sort of a look on his face. His eyes had seemed to become unfocused then as if his thoughts were not on the present but somewhere else, in the past, in the life he could not remember.

And that was what she wanted—wasn't it?

Wasn't it?

Or was it?

She needed him to know what had happened between them before she could even start to have a hope of asking him for help. Before she could tell him about Daisy and the vital operation the baby needed. And if kissing her—more than kissing her—jolted his memories back into place then why not go along with it, at least for now?

'That's better,' she heard Andreas murmur and knew that, in spite of herself, the direction of her thoughts had brought her closer to him, made her body soften against his. And when his hand slid under her chin again, lifting her mouth to his once more, she had no strength to fight him.

Or, rather, she had no strength to fight herself. This was what she wanted after all. There was no way she could deny it any longer. This was what her awakened senses demanded, what they yearned for. She needed his mouth on hers, needed the hard, intimate pressure, the warm, slick exploration of his tongue. And as his hands began to move over her she knew she needed that too. Everything inside her that had been folded tightly in on itself, closed off, shut away, now seemed to slowly unfurl, like a flower opening to the sun. And in just the same way that the flower instinctively turned towards the greatest, most glorious, most powerful source of heat and light, so without being able to stop herself she swayed towards Andreas, pressing herself against those caressing hands, writhing under the pleasure of his touch.

Murmurs of delight she couldn't hold back escaped her lips

in the brief moments that he allowed her to breathe and his name was a sigh on her lips, breathed into his mouth so that he swallowed down the sound as he took possession of her lips again.

'You see,' he murmured, husky and soft, letting that tormenting mouth slide along the line of her jaw so that she lifted her chin to tauten the muscles there, feeling it more intensely as he kissed his way to the most sensitive spot just under her ear. 'This is right. So right.'

One of those caressing hands had moved to her neck now, tangling in the soft hair at the base of her skull, twisting, tugging, pulling her head backwards so that he exposed the whole of her neck and the long, fine line down to her shoulder and the valley between her breasts that lay in the deep V-neckline of her dress. Becca's head swam as she felt the heat of his breath, the soft, tantalising caress of his mouth as it moved down into that warm valley of her cleavage.

'I want you…'

She felt as well as heard the words. They feathered over her skin, humid as the breath that seemed to slip inside her bra, coil around her nipples, making them tighten into stingingly aroused peaks that yearned for a touch that was harder, more forceful than a whisper of heated air.

'I want you,' he said again.

And she wanted him. The need was a heavy pulse between her legs, a throbbing demand from every aching nerve end along her body. Who cared if the sensual memories hidden in Andreas' numbed brain took him back into the past they had shared? So what if the touch of her lips, the taste of her skin, woke him to a recollection of exactly who she was and what she had been to him? He had to remember some time, it was inevitable. And surely it was better that he remembered sooner rather than later so that the truth was out in the open and they could renegotiate from there?

But the real truth was that she couldn't stop herself. And as her body rediscovered the pleasures she had thought she had forgotten she knew that she wanted this. She *needed* it. She had been dying inside for almost a year for the loss of it.

This *was* right, her sensual instincts told her. This was what had always been right between them. In Andreas' arms she had always felt that she was where she belonged, that she had come home. This was the one thing that had never gone wrong between them; the thing that had still been there at the end when it seemed that everything else had gone, been destroyed by hatred, distrust and cruel rejection.

Rejection.

The word was a cold, hard, vicious blade that slashed through the heated delirium inside her head, breaking open her sensual fantasies and making the wild, foolish dreams evaporate, once more letting in the icy winds of reality and self-preservation.

What was she doing courting that rejection all over again? Could she go through that pain, that loss, that terrible, terrible devastation a second time? It had almost destroyed her the first time and yet here she was risking her heart, her soul, all over again.

She couldn't do this just for the pleasure, for the physical satisfaction it would bring. It would destroy her if she did. But Andreas could. He had already done so once and she had no doubt that he could do it again. Whether his memory returned or not, he could take her, use her, take all she had to give and then turn and walk away without a backward look.

And the dread that brought made her stiffen against his stroking hands.

'Andreas…' she tried but he wasn't listening. His mouth was still caressing her skin, his hands moving down over the soft blue skirt of her dress, over her hips, inching the material upwards as they did so.

'Andreas—stop!'

Driven by rising panic, she twisted away from him sharply, fear giving her strength she didn't know she possessed. The force of her reaction took her halfway across the room before she came to a halt and was able to face him, eyes wide, her breath coming in raw, uneven gasps.

She couldn't really see him, her gaze was blurred and unfocused, and she was grateful for the way that hid the reality of his expression from her.

'No,' she said breathlessly, struggling for control. 'No, it isn't right—it can't be right! This isn't going to happen—I won't let it happen.'

'*You* won't let it happen?'

Andreas' voice was a cynical drawl and one dark eyebrow lifted in mocking response to her outburst.

'Lady, you are fooling yourself if you expect me to believe that.'

'Of course I expect you to believe it! I—'

'But I don't. I don't believe a word that comes from your lovely mouth.'

'You—you don't?'

Andreas shook his head in firm response to her shaken question. Her vision had cleared now and she could see his face. Immediately she wished she had the comfort of the protective blur back when she saw his burning eyes fixed on her face in a look of pure scorn.

'You expect me to believe your cowardly little protest when I know the truth?'

'Oh, so you're a mind-reader now?'

No—defiance was a bad move. She saw it in his face, in the way that those beautifully shaped lips clamped tightly together over some savage retort that he had hastily caught back.

'I don't need to read *minds*,' he bit out. 'But I am pretty good at understanding body language. Unfortunately for you. Because your body was speaking the truth—the truth you're now trying to pretend never happened.'

'I— No— I'm not pretending!'

'You're either pretending now or you were then—you can't have it both ways, Becca. So which one is it?'

Oh, how did she answer that? How did she tell him something that explained her behaviour and yet didn't give her away completely? The only thing she knew was that she couldn't let him believe that she had simply been leading him on—that was the course most likely to have Andreas demand that she leave right here and now. And then she would never be able to help Daisy. And saving Daisy's life was uppermost in her mind right now.

'All right—I'm sorry…'

She actually held out her hand towards him, as if pleading with him, begging him to take it. But the way that he watched the gesture, regarding it coldly with blank and unresponsive eyes, brought her up sharp. Becca felt as if she might just as well have slammed her hand against a hard brick wall and had to struggle to resist the temptation to snatch it back and cradle it against her as if his wintry response had actually hurt her physically.

'I'm sorry…' she said again, fighting to find something she could say.

'You said that already,' Andreas flung back, folding his arms across the broad expanse of his chest as his dark head went back, black eyes searing over her in a look of supreme contempt as he looked down his straight slash of a nose at her. 'Try something else. Sorry for what?'

'For—for overreacting.'

It was the only thing she could think of. The truth—or at least as close to the truth as she dared to go—seemed to be the only way to handle this. In any case, the partial truth was the only thing she trusted herself to be able to say without making it painfully plain that she was actually lying.

She'd hoped that that would be enough but, from Andreas' set, unyielding expression, it was far from adequate. If anything those folded arms tightened expressively and his upper lip actually curled in an expression of arrogant scorn.

She was going to have to try harder to convince him.

'I—I do w-want you.'

Really, there was no point in denying that. Her response to him had made it only too plain and she would only incense him further if she tried to pretend otherwise. If there was one thing that Andreas hated it was lies. A miserably cold, sneaking shiver went down her spine as she recalled the one time she had tried to keep the truth from him. She hadn't actually *lied* but she might as well have done. The fallout had been as bad as if she had.

'Then what are you doing over on the other side of the room while I'm here?'

'Because—because…'

Desperation brought inspiration and she hurried the words out, needing them to be said so that she could see if they had the effect she hoped for—the effect she prayed they would.

'Because you were right—it isn't a good idea. It isn't sensible…'

Andreas rolled his eyes in an expression of exasperation.

'And we must always be sensible, mustn't we?'

'Well, you've just had a terrible accident.'

'So now you're back to being my nurse again. I told you I hate a fuss…'

'I'm not making a fuss! I'm trying to be careful—for your sake as much as mine.'

That caught him unawares, bringing his head up in a rush.

'Me? What do I…?'

'You have amnesia.'

Becca spoke the words as slowly and as emphatically as she dared. She needed to get this through to him. If she did, then she might have a chance of staying, of working things out. Of waiting until his memory came back. And then she might have a chance of asking him to help Daisy.

'I know I have amnesia,' Andreas snarled. 'I can't forget that I do! Everything else I try to remember and I can't. The fact that I can't remember…'

He slammed the heel of his palm into his forehead with a brutal thumping sound that made her flinch inside.

'That's what I can't forget.'

'Oh, don't—please don't. Can't you see that this is why it has to be this way—because you can't take the risk?'

'You mean you can't—'

'No—you!'

Shaking her head violently, Becca took a single involuntary step towards him, then the look in his eyes, the dangerous way they flashed made her reconsider hastily. Abruptly she came to a halt again, only metres away from him, but the expanse of polished wooden floor now seemed like a wide, gaping chasm, one she knew they could never really ever bridge.

'You're the one who has the most to lose here if we—if we…'

'Lose?'

His harsh crack of laughter had no humour in it.

'From where I'm standing, I get what I want. The only thing that's interested me—excited me—since I woke up from that damn coma.'

'The only…' Becca whispered, unable to believe what she had heard. 'Me?'

'You,' Andreas confirmed roughly, with a brusque inclination of his head. 'Who did you think I meant? I was talking about excitement and pleasure—passion—something that makes life seem like it's worth living after all and not just the huge empty space where my mind—my memories—used to be. And you—you say we have to be sensible.'

He spat the word out as if it was a vile epithet.

Twice Becca opened her mouth, trying to find an answer for him, and both times her voice failed her, managing only a pathetic squeak that didn't even form a syllable, never mind a whole word.

Go to him, the irrational, emotional part of her brain was screaming. Go to him and accept what he's offering—while he's offering it. You want that excitement—you need that passion—you could enjoy—oh, dear God, more than enjoy—that pleasure. What are you doing, standing here when…?

'But we do.'

Becca couldn't believe she'd actually said what she had. Until she'd actually heard the words spoken out loud she had no idea that she had even planned to say them. She certainly hadn't thought about them rationally. She didn't even *want* to say them. But she had to. There was no other way to handle this.

'We do have to be sensible. At least you do.'

'Don't hide behind excuses. For some reason you won't admit, you're scared and you're trying to run…'

'Oh, no. No, I'm not.'

At least this time her voice had the conviction of truth. She couldn't run away. If she did she would let Macy and Daisy down. She saw Andreas' proud head go back, his eyes narrowing assessingly.

'You don't know what might have happened in your life—what you might…might find out when your memory comes back. Things that could change the way you feel about everything.'

'About you?'

Andreas' tone was sceptical.

'I doubt very much that anything could change the way I'm feeling—the hunger that's eating me up inside.'

It was purely a physical hunger—a sexual hunger—that he was talking about, Becca reminded herself miserably. There was nothing emotional about it at all. And he probably spoke the truth. Nothing had ever lessened the savage desire he had always had for her. Even when he had hated her most, he had still wanted her. The first and last thing he had done in their short-lived marriage had been to take her to bed.

But she knew just how much things would change if—when—he knew the truth about the way their relationship had ended. And she couldn't bear to think of what might happen then.

'Then—then what harm can it do to wait? You know what they say about anticipation adding to the pleasure…'

'On that point, you might be right.'

'You know I am.'

She didn't know quite how she'd done it, but somehow she'd managed to put a flirtatious note into her voice. And as she saw Andreas' expression change, the dark tension easing from his face, his eyes, she didn't know whether to feel relief or a terrible sense of fear at the thought of what she was building up for herself in the future. She might be able to persuade him now, to make him ease up, relax a little. But when his memory returned and he found out the truth, then...

Her blood turned cold at just the thought.

But she had no other possible route she could take. If she was to help Daisy at all, she had to do it this way. It was either that or leave the tiny girl to die. And that wasn't going to happen, not if she could possibly do anything to stop it. She would do whatever she had to do now, and take the consequences later when, inevitably, it all blew up in her face.

She was forced to acknowledge to herself that the thing she both most feared and most hoped for was all tangled up so that she couldn't possibly extricate one part of it from the other. Before she could ask for his help, Andreas needed to regain his memory and so she had to stay here until that happened. But when he did get his memory back he would also remember who she was and the way they had parted and then all hell would break loose.

And the real problem was that she was having to fight herself as well as Andreas. The truth was that she wanted to be in his arms as much as he wanted her there. She wanted his kisses, his touch...

Whatever else had died between them, the burning passion had not. It had brought them together, rushed them into bed, into marriage, and it was still there. It still blazed white-hot between them. Andreas had only to touch her and she went up in flames. But it hadn't been enough to hold them together before—and it wouldn't be enough now. Andreas might give her body the most glorious pleasure she had ever known but he had also broken her heart and sexual ecstasy was not enough to compensate for the pain and desolation that had followed. Andreas had been the love of her life and with every day—every hour—she spent with him she risked subjecting herself to that heartbreak all over again.

'All right.'

It was the last thing she expected Andreas to say so she actually felt her jaw drop a little when he spoke, her eyes blinking sharply in shock.

'All right?' she managed and got an unsmiling nod in response.

'We'll wait—a while. You could be right and the delay— the anticipation—will whet my appetite. I reckon you'll be worth waiting for.'

If he expected an answer to that, then he was going to be disappointed, Becca admitted to herself. There wasn't a single word she could find in her head, or form on her tongue. All she could manage was an incoherent little sound that might or might not have been agreement.

'But I won't wait for ever. I'm not a patient man, Becca. When I see something I want—I go for it.'

'I—understand.'

How could she not understand? She knew exactly what he meant; exactly how he was. Hadn't she been on the receiving end of all his forceful charm, his potent sexuality, once before? When Andreas Petrakos saw something he wanted he got it—no question.

And as if to prove it, to verify her thoughts, Andreas suddenly lifted a hand and crooked one finger in the most arrogant, supremely confident gesture, beckoning her to come to him. And from the look on his face he had no doubt that she would obey.

He was right. She could explain to herself, justify her actions, by saying that she was playing it safe, treading carefully. But if she did she would be lying to herself, stark honesty forced her to admit. She obeyed Andreas' autocratic summons, moving across the floor to him without a word or hesitation simply because she had no choice. She *had* to go to him; she didn't have the strength to resist. And as his arms came round her again she knew she was lost, lifting her face for his kiss even before he had bent his dark head towards hers.

The kiss made what little remained of her thought processes swoon. It seemed to draw out her very essence, heart and soul, taking them into his possession until she felt that she would be nothing without him, unable to function, unable even to exist on her own. She was floating, drifting, with no sense of direction or thought.

'So you'll stay,' Andreas murmured, his voice low and sensual, rich with total confidence, total conviction that he was going to get his way.

'Yes.'

There was nothing else that she could say but even as she spoke Becca had the terrible feeling of water, deep, dark and cold, closing over her head, drowning her. But there was no hope of turning back.

'Yes,' she said, soft and low. 'Yes, I'll stay.'

# CHAPTER SIX

'SO HOW long, exactly, did you foresee this "being sensible" to last?'

Andreas stretched lazily in the sunshine, noting with satisfaction that the rawness of torn muscles, the ache of bruising, was easing more with each day. If only he could say the same about the blank space where part of his memory should be. That and the burn of frustration that nagged at him all day, every day, simply because Becca was around.

At least the last few days had given his body a chance to heal physically. He would never admit it but the accident had taken more out of him than he liked, so spending time showing Becca around the island, taking her to his favourite restaurant, walking along the shore, had filled in the days of convalescence and stopped him climbing the walls with boredom.

Becca stirred her head against the cushions of the sun lounger next to him and opened those blue-green eyes in a look of such sleepy sensuality that it had his body hardening and aching in a moment, straining against the black stretch fabric of the swimming shorts that were all he wore. She was dressed all in white today in a loose sleeveless top and cotton trousers that were cut off short, revealing her slender calves and ankles.

'How do you feel?' she asked and in spite of her attempt to look relaxed he could hear the note of constraint in her voice that was always there when he moved the conversation away from the ordinary, everyday subjects they talked about.

Just what was it she was so uptight about? Was there something she was hiding? Something she didn't want him to know? It gave him the most disturbing feeling that the one person in the world he felt really comfortable with—someone he knew he had shared the missing part of his life with—might be deliberately holding something back from him.

'I feel fine! Never better!' he snapped, the edgy feeling getting the better of him, and he watched the change in her eyes, the way that the warm sensuality died, turning instead to a careful, defensive distance. Silently he cursed himself for his over-hasty reaction.

'And the doctor said you were OK at your check-up this morning?'

'You mean he didn't give you a full report? After all, your role as my nurse seems to be the only one you're interested in fulfilling.'

'I thought you'd done away with that idea? To tell you the truth...' Becca pulled herself up against the wooden back of the lounger so that she was sitting upright and looking him straight in the face '...I'm not at all sure what you want from me.'

'You know only too well what I want.'

Andreas made no attempt to disguise the blatantly sexual double meaning behind his words.

'How I want you—where I want you.'

There was that wary flicker in her eyes again. A momentary glance into his face and then away, fast, to stare out at the horizon. She affected an intense interest in the ocean that lapped lazily against the shore beyond the sunlit terrace.

'I thought we—agreed to take that slowly.'

'We agreed to be sensible. It's not the same thing.'

'To me it is. For one thing, I have no idea whether you have anyone else in your life—and you can't promise that you don't,' she pointed out.

'But if we're a couple…'

'I've been in England a long time…' Becca hedged.

So that was it. They'd been apart, and she wasn't sure she could trust him. That he could understand.

'There isn't anyone else in my life.'

'And you can swear to that, can you?'

'Well, for one thing I think she'd have turned up by now if there was someone. She'd have heard of my accident. And for another, then Leander would have told me if I was married or anything stupid like that.'

Now what had he said to make her mouth tighten as if against something she'd thought better of saying? And her eyes had moved to the swimming pool, studying the water there as if she had never seen anything like it before.

'And I doubt if Medora is going to sit back and watch me make a fool of myself over you if she knows I was committed to anyone else.'

'So that's what you think you're doing, is it?' Becca's tone was tart. 'Making a fool of yourself?'

'How the hell should I know?' Irritation at the way she wouldn't look at him, as much as at her tone, roughened the edges of the words. 'I don't know if I've behaved—or felt—this way before.'

He *couldn't* have felt this way before, he'd decided that already. If he'd ever felt this heat of desire for a woman, the sort of burning hunger that made his days impossible to get through without being with her, seeing her, touching her, and turned his nights into sweat-drenched, sleep-deprived endurance tests, then surely he would remember *that*?

And how could he wipe away the memory of the brief moments of restless sleep that he'd finally managed? Sleep in which his dreams were so vivid, so hot, so passionately erotic that they were almost unendurable. And yet waking to find that they had only been a dream had left him gasping for breath and struggling to regain any trace of his lost control.

He couldn't have forgotten those feelings. Not if he had ever experienced anything like them for anyone else before.

'And I believe that in England you have some saying about kettles and pans…'

'Pots,' Becca corrected automatically, still using that stiff little voice that scraped over his nerves. 'Pot calling the kettle black—so what has that got to do with me?'

She sounded so English, so controlled, so *sensible* that it set his teeth on edge and made him determined to shake her out of that mood. He wanted back the Becca he had seen under the prim and proper exterior on the day of her arrival. The sensual Becca, the hotly responsive Becca. The Becca whose soft, full mouth had felt so wonderful, tasted so delicious under his. Whose firm, high breasts had fitted so perfectly into his hands, the tight nipples pushing against the palms. The Becca who would have been in his bed there and then if she hadn't had ridiculous, apprehensive, *sensible* second thoughts.

'You say you don't know if there's anyone else in my life but I could say the same about you.'

'About me?'

That edgy look was back, making him think even more of words like guilt and concealment—and *lies*.

'Are *you* a free agent? Is there anyone else in your life?' he pressed.

'Oh…'

For a second she looked blank, and then he noticed that her white teeth were digging into the soft fullness of her lower lip, worrying at the soft skin that only moments before he had been imagining kissing.

'Becca?' Suspicion darkened his voice on the question.

Was this what she wasn't telling him? Was the reason she wanted to be 'sensible' because there was another man in her world? Someone she didn't want to tell him about?

'Is there—?'

'No!' she said firmly and hastily—too firmly, too hastily so that instead of putting his mind at rest it put him more on edge than ever. 'No—there's no one.'

'Are you sure?'

That brought her head round, dark hair flying, chin coming up defiantly as she met his assessing stare head-on.

'Of course I'm sure!' she declared. 'There is no man in my life but you!'

It was what he most wanted to hear, so why did he sense something like the crawl of small, icy feet down his spine in spite of the heat?

'Good,' he said, reaching out to touch a hand to her cheek and hold her there, sea-coloured eyes locked with black. 'Just make sure it stays that way. I have exclusive rights to my women. You're mine and only mine…'

Under the touch of his fingers her face jerked just once as if in rejection of his comment. Her eyes opened wide and that determined little chin lifted even higher.

'You don't have any rights to me—not yet.'

'Not *yet*,' Andreas agreed, a slow, appreciative smile curling his mouth. She was gorgeous when she was like this— wonderfully sexy with the mutinous spark that lit those fantastic eyes, the wash of colour that flooded her cheeks. 'I know—we're taking this slowly…being *sensible*.'

He drawled out the word deliberately, putting every ounce of contempt he could into each syllable.

'But not for long. I could make you forget about that need for caution you think is so important.'

Another jerk of her chin, a lift of her smoothly arched brows, challenging the truth of his assertion, making his smile widen ever more.

'You know I could,' he murmured softly, leaning even closer so that his mouth was just inches away from the soft, rebellious pout of her lips. 'It would only take a minute. Not even that.'

She had frozen now, nothing moving but her eyes as they watched him warily, waiting to see what he would do next.

'All I'd have to do is to lean forward, just the tiniest little bit…'

He suited the action to the words, only just catching the tiny faint sound of her swiftly indrawn breath as he did so. Her eyes widened just a little bit more but she stayed where she was, though the pink tip of her tongue slid out and slicked over her lower lip in an uneasy, betraying gesture.

The movement and the slight film of moisture it left on her mouth was a temptation that Andreas couldn't resist. He'd waited too long for the taste of her mouth on his all over again. He wanted it again and he wanted it now.

Reaching up a hand, he curled it round the back of her head, fingers sliding into the silky dark hair, cupping the fine bones of her skull as he drew her near to him and took her mouth. Her lips were as soft and delicious as they had been before and she yielded to him with a soft murmur that made his senses give a hard, painful kick in response.

To hell with being sensible. This was what he wanted.

What he needed. Her mouth opened under his and with a sense of triumph he moved in closer.

And felt the faint, unmistakable shiver that ran through her body as she fought for control. It was there and gone again in the space of a heartbeat but he had felt it and recognised it for what it was.

He could kiss her out of it, he knew that. It wouldn't take much; she would be his if he only insisted, pressed a little more. But it was the fact that she had reacted in that way, that she still felt that restraint she talked about that stopped him dead in his tracks. She was still determined to keep him at arm's length for her own personal reasons. And that realisation destroyed the sensual mood completely.

With a savagely muttered curse in his own language he wrenched his mouth away from hers, pulling his head back to stare down into her dark, shocked eyes.

'Andreas…' Becca began and the shake on the sound of his name was the last straw.

Swearing brutally, he tore himself away from her, taking several swift, strong and almost blind strides across the tiled surround of the pool and diving head first into the cool water, plunging way down into the clear blue depths, driving himself as hard and as far as he could.

Becca watched him go through eyes that were blurred with sudden tears. She knew what had made him react like this, the tiny shudder of panic she hadn't been able to control, but that didn't mean that she understood quite what state of mind had influenced him. Was it fury—cold-blooded anger at the way that she was still determined to hold on to the idea of being sensible? Or was it an attempt to cool himself off literally?

Whatever his feelings were, they were wild and fierce and he was having to fight to bring them under control. That much was obvious from the way he was powering down the swimming pool, face down, black hair clinging to his skull, muscular arms and legs pushing him through the clear water at a speed that gave Becca a momentary pang of concern for any possible after-effects from the accident. The bruises from his injuries might be fading, but was it safe for him to subject himself to such a physical test?

But even as the worry crossed her mind she saw that Andreas was already slowing his furious pace. He eased up, continued to swim for a while but at a much more sedate speed and eventually came back to the side of the pool just beside where she stood. Slicking back his soaking black hair with a powerful hand, he supported himself on strong arms as he trod water, looking up into her watchful face, dark eyes narrowed against the sun.

'And now I suppose you're going to say that, as my nurse, you can't approve of my behaviour just now?' he commented cynically. 'Isn't this your cue to tell me that it wasn't at all sensible—?'

'I wouldn't dare say anything of the sort!' Becca flung back at him, the uncanny way that he had almost read her mind unsettling her even more. She might have been thinking it but she certainly wasn't saying it, not knowing the reaction she would undoubtedly get.

She just hoped that Andreas would believe that irritation was uppermost in her mind and so accept it as the explanation for the way her voice went up and down in the most embarrassing way. She had felt bad enough a moment earlier and the thought that he might recognise her response as one of purely physical awareness of the body floating lazily in the water, the tense muscles in the hard forearms, the glisten of water drops on the bronzed skin was more than she could handle right now. The drenched black hair clung so close to his scalp that it formed a severe frame for those devastating features, emphasising wide, carved cheek-bones, the long, straight nose, hard jaw and almost shockingly softly sensual mouth. Her pulse was already racing in double time, making her heart catch tight in her throat. She couldn't take another of his sensual onslaughts on her, any more of those devastating, breath-stealing, soul-destroying kisses.

'I'm glad to hear it,' Andreas retorted drily, hauling himself up onto the side of the pool and sitting on the edge with his long legs dangling over the side, feet in the water. 'Because you seem so determined to revert to the nursing role that I was beginning to wonder if perhaps we ought to discuss your salary.'

'I don't want that!'

Sheer horror and the knowledge of just what she was hiding pushed the words from Becca's mouth in an urgent rush. Scrambling down beside him so that she was on a level with him, she caught hold of his arm, looking earnestly into his face.

'You don't have to pay me! After all, I'm not doing anything to earn it…'

Her voice trailed off in shivering embarrassment as she felt a tide of heated blood flood her face, making her cheeks burn at the thought of the other way that her words might be interpreted.

'I didn't mean… You don't have to pay me to…'

Oh, hell, she was making matters so much worse. Her tongue seemed to have swollen to twice its size, tangling up in her mouth so that she couldn't get another syllable out, either to explain or to apologise. And the lazy smile that crossed that hard-boned face only made matters worse, the laughter in his eyes mocking her confusion and embarrassment.

'Not pay perhaps, but I have a reputation for generosity to my mistresses.'

*My mistresses.*

If he had fired an arrow straight at her heart, piercing it brutally, it couldn't have had a more painful effect than just hearing him speak so casually.

*My mistresses.*

That was all he thought of her as; all she would ever be; all he wanted her to be. Andreas only thought of her as someone with whom he wanted a sexual relationship—a mistress, nothing more. And he had said mistresses—using the plural. Which meant that he thought in terms of more than one relationship, of women who had come before her and... Her throat closed up, making it difficult to breathe... Women who would come after her.

And since their wedding day?

There was the burn of hot tears at the backs of her eyes as she forced herself to face an even less bearable thought. The idea that once he had rejected her, he had replaced her with someone else—maybe more than one someone else. How soon after her broken-hearted departure had he brought a new woman into the house that was supposed to have been her marital home? How quickly had he found someone new to warm his bed, fill his days?

How many of them had there been since she had been driven away from him?

The tears that stung at her eyes welled up even more, fighting for release. And with grim determination Becca fought them back, struggling to force them down, refusing to let them fall. But she could only manage the control she needed by gritting her teeth, refusing to blink, swallowing as hard as she could.

'Becca?'

She wished she could say something—anything to make

him look away. Preferably something light and throwaway
that would distract him, make him laugh, direct that too intent,
too searching scrutiny somewhere else. How could she
recover her composure, get back her self-possession when he
was watching her as if she was some particularly fascinating
specimen under a microscope? One he wanted to dissect and
analyse completely.

She knew that her cheeks were burning painfully. The
struggle to fight back the tears had added to the already embarrassed colour in her skin. Mortified beyond bearing, she
lifted a hand and brushed it across her face, praying that the
small gesture would at least break the focus of that concentrated stare.

'You're hot,' Andreas said quietly, the note of concern in
his words almost destroying her completely. 'And no wonder
when you're wearing too much clothing.'

If there had been the slightest trace of a sexual intonation
in what he'd said, anything that had made her think that he
was deliberately putting a double edge onto the phrase, then
Becca knew she would have totally lost control. But the note
of genuine concern destroyed her composure in a totally different way.

'Why don't you put on a swimming costume and spend
some time in the pool? You're clearly not used to this sort of
heat and the water would cool you down.'

It wasn't the heat of the sun that was disturbing her, Becca
admitted to herself. It was the subtler, more sensual warmth
of his body so close to hers that she could smell the intimate,
intensely personal scent of his skin, topped with the tang of
the water that still clung to it. That and the heat of her own
response, the honeyed sense of need that flooded her body,
pooling moistly at the junction of her thighs.

A swim would be just what she needed. It would ease the burn of hunger, soothe the ache in her body. But there was one very practical problem.

'I don't have a swimming costume,' she managed, casting a longing glance at the cool, fresh water as it lapped against the clean blue tiles of the pool. 'I—never thought that I would need one when I came here. And to be honest, I never thought I'd stay this long.'

She could have bitten out her tongue as soon as she'd spoken, realising too late how close she'd come to giving away the truth that she was not really the person he'd believed her to be. But Andreas hadn't noticed the slip, too intent on his own train of thought.

'That's not a problem. I can soon provide you with a costume. There's one in the pool house over there.'

A wave of his hand indicated the small stone-formed building that provided a changing room and a shower for those who used the pool.

'I saw it hanging up there when I went in this morning. It should fit you. Why don't you go and try it on?'

And come back here, wearing it?

Becca's mind quailed at the thought. Just the idea of sitting here beside him, lying in the sun or swimming in the pool close to him in some sleek, close-fitting Lycra costume made the tingling worse, bringing it close to the sensation of an electrical shock running over her skin. If someone had left it here then it was probably one of those mistresses he had spoken of. In which case, was it likely that the costume was anything more than a few skimpy pieces of material, precariously held up by a couple of shoestring straps?

And yet the idea of getting away for a moment, going into the pool house to be by herself, as she had hardly been at any moment over the last three days, except when she had retired to bed, suddenly seemed such an appealing idea. She could hide away there for a while, regain her composure, gather her strength. And then maybe she'd be able to cope much better than she had been doing until now.

'I'll do that,' she said, fighting with herself to make sure that she got to her feet slowly, trying desperately not to make it look as if she was running away even though she knew deep in her heart that that was what she was doing.

'I'll be back in a minute.'

And the costume? she asked herself as she padded on bare feet across the stone-paved terrace, heading for the pool house. Well, if it fitted—and was in any way modest—then she might risk it.

She'd make up her mind when she saw it.

But when she saw the pale lavender swimming costume hanging on a peg in the small changing room the effect of it was like a sudden blow to her heart, stilling its beat and leaving her standing staring in blank and stunned disbelief, unable to think at all.

It couldn't be. It just couldn't be, was the phrase that repeated over and over inside her head, making the real world fade from her awareness into a buzzing, whirling haze in which the only real thing was the sleek, small item of clothing before her.

'It can't,' she said, shaking her head in shock. 'It *can't* be.'

Because the costume she now held in shaking hands was the one that she had worn herself on the single day she had spent in the villa as Andreas' wife.

# CHAPTER SEVEN

IT STILL fitted her.

That was a shock. She knew she had lost weight in the ten and a half months since her wedding and that she was no longer the relaxed, happy-go-lucky person she had been before she had met and married Andreas Petrakos.

But the lavender swimming costume still fitted almost perfectly. There was so much Lycra in the material that it clung to her new, more slender shape, the low neck exposing softer curves, the high-cut legs revealing slender hips and thighs that had been so much more rounded when she had first worn it.

Looking at herself in the full-length mirror that hung on the wall of the changing room, Becca smoothed hands that were none too steady over the clinging material and tried to remember the Becca who had looked into the same mirror not quite a year before. Then her eyes had been sparkling with delight and the sensual satisfaction of having just made wild, abandoned, passionate love with her brand-new husband. And there had been a wide smile on her mouth that she had felt sure was going to be there for ever and that nothing would ever erase it.

She couldn't have been more wrong.

Barely two hours later she had been on her way home, leaving her married life lying in pieces behind her.

'Love!' Andreas' harsh voice, with its cruelly cynical emphasis on that vital word, echoed down from the past, sounding so loud and clear inside her thoughts that she almost believed for a moment that he had come into the room and thrown the word at her.

'I don't love anyone—least of all you! I doubt if I'm capable of the feeling...'

They had arrived on the island late in the afternoon after the flight from England. Becca was still floating on a cloud of happiness after the delight of their wedding, the bliss of the thought of being Andreas' wife. And she truly was his wife. He had wasted no time in making sure of that. They had been barely through the door before he had carried her upstairs to his bedroom, stripped her of the elegant trouser suit she had worn for travelling and made passionate love to her with all the ardour and the heat of which he was capable.

Later, when Andreas had reluctantly been obliged to go to his office to deal with a fax that had come through unexpectedly, Becca had changed into the lavender-coloured one-piece swimming costume and headed for the pool.

'I'll join you there as soon as I can,' he'd promised.

He was much longer than she had anticipated. She was tired and bored, and thinking of getting dressed again before he came back onto the terrace where he stood, hands on hips, his face almost white with some fierce emotion that made his eyes glitter like polished jet.

'Get dressed.'

It was an order, an autocratic command delivered with such savagery that her blood ran cold, icy pins and needles prickling her skin in spite of the heat of the day.

'I want to talk to you.'

The words had barely left his lips before he turned on his

heel and walked away, either not hearing or deliberately turning a deaf ear to her shaken question, her nervous request for an explanation as to his sudden change in mood.

She hardly dared take the time to dry herself thoroughly, discarding the swimming costume and hauling on jeans and a T-shirt, pushing her feet into flip-flops, barely pausing for breath as she almost ran from the pool house and into the office, where Andreas was standing by the window, silhouetted against the setting sun, as he waited for her.

'What's happened? Is there something wrong?'

'You tell me.'

There was nothing of the ardent, caring husband in his tone; nothing of the passionate lover who had torn himself so reluctantly from her arms and from their bed just a short time before. What could have happened to have changed his mind and his mood so terribly?

'Andreas? What's happened? What's this about?'

'You tell me what it's about. Tell me about Roy Stanton.'

He flung the name at her like a weapon, watching through narrowed eyes so that he caught the way she flinched, the sudden step she took backwards in uncontrolled shock.

'So you do know the name, then?'

It was too late to deny it. Her reaction had already given her away.

'How—how did you...?'

'How did I find out?'

An arrogant flick of his wrist tossed away the question as so obvious that it didn't need an answer.

'An investigation into these things is easy to arrange.'

'You—had me *investigated*!' She sounded as appalled as she felt. And she felt even worse when Andreas shrugged off that question too, with even less concern than he had given the first.

'I have every right to know what my prospective wife is doing with the small fortune I've given her. And I do not believe that you have the right to judge my actions when what you did was give that money to some other man. Or are you claiming that that's not true?'

'No…'

Becca sank down onto one of the wooden benches in the changing room as the bitter memories of that day took all the strength from her legs. Andreas hadn't given her a chance to explain. He had bombarded her with questions like some brutal counsel for the prosecution, demanding answers to a new one even while she was still stumbling over the answer to the last. And all the time she had been bound by the promise she had made to Macy. The promise to her newly discovered sister. The sister she had never known she had until just a few short weeks before.

At first Macy had wanted nothing to do with her but then suddenly she had phoned, asking to meet, asking for help. But she had made Becca promise that she wouldn't tell a soul.

'No, I'm not claiming that.'

'You gave this man money?' Andreas had thundered. 'All the money I gave you, by the look of it.'

'You said it was mine!'

'You know damn well that I gave that to you to buy your wedding dress and anything else you wanted for—'

'Are you saying that the dress I wore wasn't good enough?' Becca rushed in, jumping to the defensive in a panic as she struggled to think of some explanation she could give him.

Her mind was reeling in shock at just the thought that Andreas had found out about Roy Stanton. There was no reason at all that he should even know the man's name. And so she tried to stall him, using any argument she could to distract him while she tried to work out just what was happening and how she could possibly answer him at all.

But going on the attack was the wrong move—the worst possible move of all. From being icily angry, Andreas' temper went into meltdown, blazing fierce and furious as a forest fire, engulfing everything that stood in its way. And before she knew what was happening, it seemed that *he* was accusing *her*. But of what she was not quite sure.

'The dress was fine—as far as it went. But it could have been more—should have been more…'

'Should have! So now I have to wear what you order just to make sure that—that what? That I didn't show you up by not wearing something suitable to match your status? Is that it, Andreas? Are you angry because I didn't marry you in a couture gown—a designer original? One that would show my family—your friends—how wonderfully you can provide for me? That you can give me a fortune to spend on a single dress for a single day…'

'A fortune that you gave to another man.'

'I had my reasons!'

'And what were they?'

And that simple question brought the whole argument to a crashing halt. The words died on her lips, crushed back down her throat as if someone had put a gag right over her mouth and tied it so tightly that she had no chance of saying a word in her own defence.

Because the truth was that she was gagged by her promise to Macy. She had sworn on everything she held sacred not to say a word. Not until Macy was safe. And when she had discovered that her already emotionally vulnerable half-sister was also very newly pregnant that vow had become even more important. So, even though it tore at her heart, she had to hold to that promise.

'I—can't say.'

'Can't or won't?' Andreas snarled and the savagery of his tone had her flinching back, terrified of his rage, the flames of fury that blazed in the darkness of his eyes.

'Andreas—please…'

How had this happened? How had the wonderful, blissful mood in which they'd reached the villa been turned into this terrible horror, this brutal tearing each other apart?

'It was just money…'

'My money—the money I gave you. And you gave it to him…'

And then she thought she could see what was happening. In a sudden rush of understanding, she felt she knew just why he was so angry—what had got to him so badly. She had always known about the dark shadow over Andreas' past. The fact that his mother had only married his father for the money he had, the lifestyle he could give her, and when Alexander Petrakos had lost much of his fortune through some rash and ill-advised stock-market gambling Alicia had taken off with his wealthier cousin, turning her back on her five-year-old son without a second thought.

Then later, when Andreas himself had rebuilt the Petrakos fortune so that it had more than doubled the original amount, Alicia had turned yet again and tried to come back to the son she had abandoned over twenty years before. As a result, Andreas had always been wary of being used in the same way as his father. The slightest suspicion that any woman in his life might be a gold-digger meant that she was dropped so fast she never had time to even try to change his mind.

So if Andreas thought—or even suspected—that she had married him for his money…

'Andreas, don't…' she tried again. 'It doesn't have to be this way.'

There had to be a way that she could reach him. A way that they could talk this out. If she could just calm him down, make him see that things could be put right. And then she'd talk to Macy, get her to see that she couldn't keep her promise. She had to tell Andreas—he was her husband.

'Doesn't it?'

'No—not if you love me…'

A sharp pain in her fingers jolted Becca back to the present, where, staring down at her hand, she realised that she had been twisting the stretchy material of the swimming costume round and round until it had tightened about her fingers, digging into the skin.

But the tight physical pain was as nothing when compared to the one in her heart as she remembered Andreas' reaction to her stumbling attempt to put things right, or at least bring about a truce between them.

'Love!' Andreas' harsh bark of laughter had been cruel and totally without any humour in it. 'Love? Who brought love into this?'

'But you—I—you married me…'

'Not for love!' he flung the word in her face. 'I don't love anyone—least of all you! I doubt if I'm capable of the feeling. I married you for sex—for that and nothing else. No other woman has ever made me feel as hot as you do.'

It was as if some freezing iceberg had suddenly enclosed her so that she could see and hear but she was incapable of moving and, for now at least, the terrible cold had deadened all feeling so that she was numb right through to the soul. Even her heart hardly seemed to be beating at all.

'S-sex?'

'Yes—sex. That thing we just enjoyed upstairs.'

'I didn't enjoy it.'

'Liar.'

She wouldn't have enjoyed it, couldn't have enjoyed it if she'd known that he had been using her as cold-bloodedly and cruelly as it now seemed. If their whole marriage had been based on a lie and not the real love she believed it to be.

'You had no right…' she began but her frozen tongue wouldn't form the words. Her lips were so stiff they felt as if they were carved from wood.

'No right to what?'

Andreas' expression was carved from a similar block of ice as the one that seemed to enclose her. His jaw was taut and rigid, eyes freezing black pools.

'To marry me if you felt that way. You have nothing to give me!'

'Nothing!'

His laughter was so hard that it seemed to splinter in the air around her, making her wince away from the shattered fragments that threatened her face.

'Take a look around you, *agape mou.*'

One long fingered hand waved in a gesture that took in the luxurious room, the beautiful pool out beyond the patio doors and the view of the sapphire-blue ocean beyond that again. 'You call this nothing?'

Nothing without love.

'Isn't this enough?'

'Quite frankly, no.'

Bitterness made her say it. Agony pushed it from her lips in a cold, tight voice that didn't sound at all like her own.

'I expected more from you.'

'You expected… Well, you can expect all you like but you'll get nothing else from me—nothing.'

'You think I'll stay for that?' she asked.

'I don't think you'll stay for anything. In fact, let's make this easy for you—let me help you on your way.'

Marching into the hall, he flung open the big wooden door, letting in the warm evening air where the shadows were now gathering.

'Andreas, you can't do this! You married me today—we—we just consummated our marriage.'

But what sort of marriage was it when the man she adored had just baldly announced that he didn't love her?

'If you divorce me then it will cost you even more...'

It was meant to bring him to his senses. To get him to see that if she was only after him for his money, then he was going the right way about making sure that she got as much as she could possibly want. Surely the thought that she would get half of his vast fortune would make him stop and think and see where he was going wrong.

*Thinking* looked like the last thing that Andreas was capable of. And stopping was obviously the last thing that was on his mind. She'd never seen him like this before in her life. She could almost see the red mist of fury behind his eyes, and his dark face was so contorted into a snarl that she barely recognised him as the man she had loved so deeply. The man she had vowed only that morning to love, honour and cherish.

The man who had vowed the same while all the time he had a lie in his heart. He hadn't meant a thing.

*'I married you for sex—for that and nothing else.'*

He didn't love her. Did she really want to be married to a man who felt that way, no matter how much she cared about him? What sort of a marriage would she be tying herself to?

'Andreas, I'll be entitled to half of everything you own—and I'll take it.'

She wanted to shock him; prayed it would bring him to his senses. Perhaps she could…

'It'll be worth it to get rid of you.'

Whirling round, he snatched up her suitcase, which still stood at the foot of the stairs where he had deposited it on their arrival. With a violent movement he tossed it out of the door and then turned back to face her, challenge stamped into every hard line of his dark, savage face.

'Now, are you going to follow it or do I have to throw you out myself?'

It was then that Becca gave up, gave in. She had no more fight left in her, and besides, she didn't know what she was fighting for.

Was she going to beg—to plead with him to let her stay? Even if she managed to convince him that she had married him because she loved him, what difference would it make? He had made his position brutally plain. He had married her for sex and that was all. He wouldn't care if she loved him— the only thing he gave a damn about was his money.

Drawing herself up to her full height, she imposed a control on her quivering mouth, her burning eyes, that she didn't know she was capable of. She didn't know how she *looked,* but she knew how she wanted him to think she *felt* and prayed she was communicating that with her demeanour, her expression. *Please* let it show in her eyes. She was determined not to let a single tear fall, no matter how bitterly they stung at the backs of her eyes, how hard she had to fight not to blink them away.

'Oh, I'm going—don't worry. There's nothing here to stay for. I think I've got all that I wanted from this relationship.'

'Oh, I'll just bet you have. But don't think you'll be able to go for any quickie divorce. There will be no annulment— I've already made sure of that.'

Something in his voice caught on the raw, bleeding edges

of Becca's heart, making her see just what was really behind the callous declaration.

He'd known already, she realised. Somehow, though God knew how, he'd found out about Roy Stanton before their marriage. And, thinking that he would trap her in a marriage that meant nothing to him, he had gone ahead and married her after all, knowing all the time that he was going to let it come to this.

Becca had no more fight left in her. All she knew was that she had to get out of here right now, before she broke down completely. If she let Andreas see how much she was hurting, then he would know that he'd won.

Somehow she made herself go past him to get to the door. The faint brush of her arm against his as she passed almost undid her, making her body run hot and then shiveringly cold as if she was in the grip of some terrible fever. She could only pray that her legs would hold up beneath her until she was actually out of the door and heading away, far, far away from the villa. She made it outside and into the warmth of the night, where, thankfully, the darkness hid the misery in her face, the tears she was fighting a losing battle to hold back.

It was then that Andreas flung his final, unbelievable comment after her.

'Well, money I'll give you—but nothing else. Not a damn thing else.'

Marching with her head down, her eyes blind, fighting a bitter little battle with herself not to give in, Becca couldn't believe what she'd heard. He couldn't believe that all she wanted was money, and if he did then why on earth, even now, would he say that if she asked for money he would give it to her?

In confusion and bewilderment she turned, forcing herself to make one last, desperate attempt. But even as she swung round, it was already too late. Andreas had stepped back into the house, and as she watched he slammed the door shut, hard and fast, in her face.

She had to have heard wrong anyway, Becca decided. He couldn't have said what she thought he'd said. It didn't make sense.

But then nothing about this whole terrible evening made sense. The day had started out so wonderfully, with so much joy, so much hope. She had been looking into a great future—and now all that potential was over, in the past. Instead, the life she was facing seemed to have nothing to offer. And the future she had dreamed of was dead and gone.

And so she'd made herself keep walking. Walking away from the marriage she'd thought she was going to have. Away from the man she'd thought she'd loved.

The man she now tried to convince herself that she hated.

She'd walked away from the house, dragging her case with her and trying to hate him. She'd made the long journey home back to her stunned family, her bewildered friends, needing to hate him if she was to survive.

And the truth was that coming back here had proved to her in the most painful way that she hadn't succeeded.

She couldn't hate Andreas, in spite of a year of trying; it just wouldn't work. She was still every bit as much in love with him as on the day that she had married him.

# CHAPTER EIGHT

ANDREAS was sick and tired of waiting.

How long had it been since Becca had headed for the pool house? And how long did it take to get into a swimming costume, for God's sake?

Or was there a problem? She had looked uncomfortable, edgy, when she had been sitting beside him on the edge of the pool. She'd definitely been too hot—and she had such fair skin...

The thought had barely formed in his mind before Andreas pushed himself to his feet from the sun lounger on which he had been relaxing and headed in the direction of the pool house himself, padding silently across the tiles on bare feet.

She was sitting on the wooden bench that ran along the white-painted wall. Her head was bent, her eyes downcast, staring at the floor, and her hands clasped together in her lap. She had changed into the costume and once again he was aware of the pallor of her skin, barely touched by the few days she had spent with him in the sun. And with the thought came a sudden vivid mental image of the two of them in bed together, her pale limbs entwined with his darker, stronger ones.

'What is it?'

Without thinking he spoke in Greek, the sudden burn of his libido too strong to allow enough thought for translation into English.

The sound of his voice brought her head up fast, sea-blue gaze locking with his in an instant. But there was something in that look that he didn't understand. Something new and different that told him without words that a change had taken place in the time she had spent away from him.

'Are you all right?'

'Yes, fine.'

The words sounded all wrong, strangely staccato and somehow unconvincing. And the smile that she turned on him flashed on and off like some neon advertising sign. As soon as it subsided, her face was stiff and unresponsive.

'Did it fit?'

It must have done—she was wearing the damn thing. So why was she sitting here, inside, instead of out in the sun?

'Well…yes…'

She gestured to herself with a hand that was not quite steady.

'I could get into it—but…'

The look in her eyes intensified, turned them into sea-deep pools under a sweep of dark, curling lashes. She seemed wary, as if unsure of how he was going to react.

Of course. She needed reassurance. She felt unsure of herself, of the way she looked.

'Stand up…let me see.'

At first he thought she was going to refuse and that she would insist on staying where she was. But then, slowly and reluctantly, she got to her feet and turned towards him. For a moment her hands fluttered nervously and then she forced them down to her sides, obviously having trouble submitting to his appraisal. Watching her, Andreas felt his heart take up a heavy, pounding beat, one that sent the blood rushing to his brain and set his thoughts swimming.

He hadn't realised quite what a spectacular body she had been hiding under the loose, floating dresses and skirts she had been wearing since she had arrived at the villa a few days before. It had been obvious that her shape was supremely feminine, curved in all the right places, but he hadn't been able to guess at *this*. If he had noticed the pallor of her skin a moment before, now he saw how the flow of her blood just beneath the surface flooded her smooth flesh with a soft pink glow that gave it a lustre like the finest pearls. Against that paleness, the gleaming darkness of her hair was shocking, especially when combined with the unique soft colour of her eyes.

Her shoulders were softly rounded, curving down to slender arms, and in the vulnerable hollow where they joined the base of her neck—one of the most entrancing parts of a woman, he had always believed—her pulse beat hard and fast, betraying the way she was feeling.

Just for a moment he caught her eyes, saw the way she was watching him and felt his own heart kick hard as her darkened gaze locked with his. Was she really so unsure of herself? He tried a smile, aiming for the encouragement he believed she needed.

'You look—beautiful.'

And he meant it. Meant it in a way that he would never have thought possible. It was as if, just for a moment, as she'd got to her feet something in the world had slipped, tilted, and then clicked back into place. But it wasn't quite the same now. Not quite as it had been before.

But for the life of him he couldn't say how.

He couldn't think about it now. He didn't *want* to think about it. What he wanted to think about was the woman who stood before him, tall and slender and so, so feminine in the clinging one-piece.

'Beautiful…'

Her legs were longer that he'd ever imagined, seeming to go on for ever from the high-cut legs of the costume, and the way that it clung to every curve, smoothed over the swell of her breasts, the neat indentation of her waist made his mouth dry with hunger. He wanted to reach for her, pull her towards him, enfold her in his arms and kiss her senseless.

Hell, he wanted to do so much more than that!

Something of what he was feeling must have shown in his face and he saw those rich lashes lift even higher as her wary eyes widened.

Her hands fluttered up again, came to rest above the scooped neckline of the costume, crossing over, covering the rich curves of her breasts and the shadowy valley between.

'No…'

His tone was sharp and, stepping forward, he caught hold of those concealing hands, pulling them away from her, gently but firmly. And although she tensed for a moment, clearly thought about resisting, she gave in and went with him, a faint sigh escaping her as her white teeth worried at the fullness of her bottom lip. A lip that he could see was trembling in spite of her efforts at control.

'No…' Andreas repeated, more softly this time. 'No, *agape mou*—never hide yourself from me. Never.'

'But—you—I…'

Her voice was just a breathless whisper and she seemed to struggle to get the words out. It wasn't just her lip that was trembling now; he could feel the faint tremors that shook the fine lines of her body as his arms came round her, supporting her when she seemed so nervous that she might actually fall.

'No…' he said again, leaning forward to press the words against her mouth. 'Never be shy with me. Why would you want to hide such loveliness, when any man would delight in seeing you—holding you…?'

'I…'

*Never be shy with me…*

Becca barely heard the words above what seemed like the sound of a million buzzing bees inside her head, humming wildly and loudly as they whirled and twisted in a crazy flying dance that made her thoughts spin, her senses blur. Andreas thought that she was trembling all over because she was *shy;* because she was apprehensive as to what the man she was with would think of her when she first exposed her body in the clinging swimming costume to his assessing gaze. And he couldn't have been more wrong.

Or, rather, he was right but in a back-to-front sort of way.

She was nervous all right, apprehensive definitely, but not for the reasons he thought. Not because it was the first time he had seen her this way, wearing so little—but because of the exact opposite. Because she knew he *had* seen her dressed this way before and she didn't know if seeing her dressed in the costume again would remind him, jar loose whatever blockage was closing off his memory of the past from the reality of today, bring him back to himself in a rush.

And she was scared stiff that he was going to repeat his be-haviour of that day and throw her out of the villa before she had a chance to talk to him, to even try to explain.

'Andreas…'

Her mouth was so dry with fear that his name had an em-barrassingly squeaky sound, and she caught herself up, swal-lowing hard to try to ease the constriction in her throat.

'Thank you...' she managed, sounding better at least, but not much.

To her astonishment Andreas shook his head, sending the black hair, still wet from his swim, flying around his head.

'*Ochi*—no again.'

Somehow his use of his own language made his voice richer, deeper, more sensual, so that Becca caught in her breath as she heard it. And when he laid a single forefinger against her lips to silence her she felt her senses swirl again but in a very different way this time. The scent of his skin filled her nostrils, tantalising her nerves. She had to fight against the urge to open her mouth just so...and let her tongue slide out to curl around it, him, know the taste of his flesh on hers.

'I am the one who should be thanking you.'

'For—for what?' Becca questioned against his hand.

'For staying.'

'But you asked me to—and I was supposed to...'

'That is not what I mean.'

Looking deep into her confused eyes, Andreas moved the restraining finger, lifting it to the middle of her forehead and tracing his way along her hairline, stroking a gentle pathway round to her temple and down along her cheek, sliding it under her chin to lift her face to his.

'Don't you know that in a way you're the person I know best? The others—Leander, Medora—I don't remember the last year I spent with them—but that doesn't matter so much to me. We are as we have always been. But you—you're the one I feel I've come to know in the days you've been here. The one I've grown closer to. And I want to be closer...so much closer...'

'Oh, don't!'

The cry escaped her in a panic, before she had even considered what she might say if he asked her to explain her reasons for the protest. She couldn't let him go on like this—couldn't…

But Andreas wasn't listening and the next moment any chance she had of saying more evaporated in a rush as those strong fingers under her chin exerted just a little bit more pressure, tilting her face up higher, coming closer to his. And his mouth came down on hers in a kiss that stole all thought away and took her senses with it.

Andreas' kiss started out slow, almost light, but in the space of a heartbeat it had moved from gentle through enticing until it got to hungry and insistent. And in spite of her fears, or perhaps because of them, Becca found that she didn't have the strength to fight him. She didn't *want* to fight him. With the realisation of how much she still loved him right at the forefront of her thoughts, she gave herself up to that kiss, melting into his arms, feeling their strength tighten around her, holding her close.

She was pressed up against him, against the warm expanse of his naked chest, with her head resting on the hardness of his shoulder, under the smooth stretch of tanned, golden skin. The black haze of hair that covered his chest was soft underneath her chin and she sighed and rubbed her face against it, feeling it tickle her. Under the clinging swimsuit her breasts tightened and stung with need, the hardened nipples pushing against the constricting cloth, and desire was a heated, pulsing pool low down in her body.

'Becca…'

Her name was a raw sound on Andreas' tongue, thick and guttural, the sound of a hunger that matched her own.

This time when he took her lips again his kiss burned and demanded, his arms crushing her to him. And Becca went willingly, the thunder of need in her heart drowning out any weak voice of attempted caution. This was what she wanted; what she needed *now*. She didn't care about the past, had no thought of the future. What she wanted was right here in the present. Hers for the taking.

And she was going to take it.

She had spent almost a year mourning the loss of this passion in her life, hating the way that world seemed cold and hard and empty without it. Now she had one chance—probably one last chance—to experience the scalding pleasure of being here, where she most wanted to be, in Andreas' arms, with his kiss crushing her mouth, his hands hot and hard on her. And it was what she most wanted in all the world.

Those powerful hands were stroking over her skin, moving down along the straight line of her spine, leaving burning trails in their wake as if his touch was actually hot enough to mark her, brand her as his for all time to come. The feel of it made her moan aloud, arching her back like a small, sensual cat that stretched into a caress.

The movement brought her right up against him, against the heated swell of his powerful erection, a potent force that she felt almost as strongly as if she were naked, there was so little clothing to come between them. Just the heat of it made her breath catch in her throat and she swayed softly, turning her whole pelvis into a caress that had him snatching in air in a rush like a drowning man.

'Becca!'

It was half protest, half encouragement and he clamped his big hands on the tight curve of her buttocks, holding her still, but keeping her pressed hard and tight against his burning flesh.

The words he muttered in her ear were in thick, rough Greek, and so incomprehensible to her, but she didn't need to know the language to understand, at the most basic, primitive level, exactly what he was saying to her. And it was something she wanted to say right back.

'I want you…'

She choked it out, the knot of need in her throat almost preventing her from finding her voice.

'Want…want…want you!'

'*Nai*…'

His response was as rough-voiced as her own, but he didn't need speech to show her he understood—and shared—the yearning that was clawing at her deep inside. With a swift, sudden tensing of the powerful muscles in his shoulders and back, he swung her off her feet and up into his arms, turning towards the still open door behind him.

'Andreas…'

A sudden rush of embarrassment at the thought of being carried through the house like this brought his name to her lips.

'What if we meet Medora—or Leander—on the way?'

But Andreas shook his head instantly, dismissing her concerns with a smile.

'We're all alone,' he told her with a deep intensity that seared all the way along every nerve path until it made her toes curl tightly in response. 'No one will bother us. And I'm sure as hell not making love to you on the pool-house floor.'

Becca barely noticed the journey through the house—up the stairs. It was only as Andreas shouldered open a door and carried her over to the bed that she realised where they were.

The master bedroom. The room that should have been theirs when they were married. The room that she had never shared with him—at least to *sleep*. Had some unconscious part of his mind directed his footsteps this way, or was it simply coincidence?

The question left her head as soon as it had entered it

because in the same moment Andreas lowered her to the floor, sliding her down the length of his body as he did so. And before her feet had actually hit the ground, he had hooked his fingers into the thin straps of the swimsuit and peeled them off her shoulders, down to her waist…

His mouth followed the same path, kissing his way from the hollow where her hungry pulse throbbed, and down over the curve of her breast, making her catch her breath in shocked delight.

'I know, *kalloni mou*…'

She could hear the smile in his voice, feel it on the lips that caressed her skin, and her own mouth curved into a wide, brilliant smile of pure delight, her head going back as she gave herself up to his skilled caress.

'It's how I feel too. How you make me feel.'

His head was moving even lower now as the little that was left of the lavender-coloured costume was eased from her, his mouth caressing every inch of the creamy skin he exposed. When he paused to let his tongue slide into the shallow indentation of her navel, drawing a sensual circle all around it, Becca could not hold back a small cry of response, her hands coming out, clutching at his hair, twisting in the black, silky strands as she held him closer to her.

He was kneeling before her now, helping her to step away from the bundle of lavender Lycra, tossing it aside without even looking, his attention totally focused on pleasuring her. The feel of his kisses over the cluster of dark hair between her legs made her writhe in sensual anticipation in the same moment that she tugged at the hair she held, wanting him closer, needing more of him, his heat against her, the scent of his body enclosing her. She wanted him everywhere, all of him, and every kiss, every touch made her hungrier, needier than ever before.

'*Anypomonos*—impatient!' Andreas laughed, the warmth of his breath feathering over her skin, stirring the curls, whispering around the sensitised opening between her legs. 'But I like that in you. I like to know that you're as hot for me as I am for you.'

'Know it…' Becca managed in a broken whisper, feeling the flood of need moisten her most intimate core, her breath catching in her throat as he began to kiss her once more—but reversing his path this time, caressing up and up until that tormenting, knowing mouth was pressed against the warm underside of one tingling, aching breast.

'Know it…' she said again, this time on a heartfelt sigh. 'I want you—need you…'

Now that he was upright again she could touch him herself, release her grip on his hair, only to explore more of his powerful male body, letting her needy fingers wander over the hot, tight skin, smooth the potent muscles that flexed and tautened beneath her touch. She didn't know where she wanted him the most, his hands at her breasts, teasing the straining nipples into harder, tighter peaks, his mouth on hers, his slick tongue probing in heated imitation of the more intimate invasion she longed for. She wanted all of him, above her, on her—*inside her.*

'These will have to go.'

It was a muttered reproach as her fingers encountered the waistband of his shorts, tugging impatiently, pushing them down, a sigh of satisfaction escaping her as she exposed the smooth warmth of his waist, the firm, muscled stretch of his buttocks. But then, as the shorts fell to the floor and he kicked them aside, not taking his attention from the devastation his hands and mouth were working on her, she let her hands slide between them, closing over the hottest, hardest part of him and smoothing her thumbs down its straining length. Her heart kicked sharply, her own hunger growing, pooling hotly between her legs as she heard his groan of anguished pleasure.

'Witch!' he muttered hoarsely, tearing his mouth away from hers to drag in a gasp of much-needed air. 'Tormentor—temptress…!'

And with a hunger too strong for care, too ardent for gentleness, he half lifted, half pushed her backwards, tumbling her down onto the bed so that she landed on the pillows with a gasp, her legs splaying out from the shock of her landing.

Andreas came down beside her before she had a chance to recover. His hands reached for her breasts, cupping them and lifting them to his mouth, his wicked tongue encircling each pouting nipple in turn, drawing erotic patterns around them, making her squirm and sigh in restless need before he concentrated all his attention on one, drawing the distended peak into his mouth and sucking softly.

At the same time his long body moved over hers, powerful, hair-roughened legs coming between her splayed ones. Pushing them even further apart, he settled himself so that the heated force of his erection just touched the central core of her body, so near and yet so far from offering her the complete fulfilment that she yearned for.

'Andreas!' she muttered in impatient protest, clenching her jaw tight over the needy words that almost escaped her. She wouldn't beg… 'Don't tease…'

'Tease, *agape mou*?' he questioned softly, a wicked smile on his lips—but one that was belied by the haze of passion that clouded his eyes, the slash of heat that scored the wide cheekbones. 'What makes you think that I am teasing? I merely want to make sure that this is what you want. That—'

'You know it's what I want!' Becca clenched her hands into

tight fists and pounded them against the rock-hard wall of his chest so close above her. Andreas grabbed at the flailing hands, holding them round the wrists and bringing them down on either side of her, holding her prisoner.

'Do you?'

'Oh, I do—I do—I do—Andreas—please…'

'Ah, well, when you ask so nicely…'

Andreas shifted slightly, pushing himself closer, almost where she wanted him…and then pausing again.

'Andreas…' Becca began warningly.

'Then who am I to deny a lady?'

'You—!'

Whatever she had been about to say was broken on a sharp cry of fulfilment as Andreas abandoned all pretence at teasing and eased himself into her waiting, welcoming body in one long, hard thrust.

'Andreas!'

This time his name was a wild, keening sound of delight, one that was pushed back into her throat as his mouth clamped down hard on hers, his strong body moving against hers, setting up an erotic rhythm that made her pulses throb in heady delight. Closing her eyes tight, the better to enjoy the feeling, she arched against him, abandoning herself to the sensual pleasure of his possession.

In the space between one frantic heartbeat and the next the smouldering embers of need sparked into wild, burning flames of hunger. Hunger that knew no restraint, allowed for no holding back. Finding themselves free, Becca's hands reached for Andreas, clamped tight over those powerful shoulders, her nails digging into the warm flesh of his back, a sob of excitement escaping her as she gave herself up to the glorious sensations they were creating between them.

It was hard, it was fast, it was hot as hell, and it was taking her closer to heaven with each burning second that passed. She could feel the incredible tension building up inside her, climbing higher and higher until she thought she would scream aloud with the pressure of need. It was there in Andreas too, in the tautness of every powerful muscle, the raw, uneven sound of his breathing, the way that his powerful hands were clamped tight around her upper arms, almost bruising the tender flesh. The peak they reached for was so close—so, so close—and yet it seemed that she would never reach it. And then Andreas bent his head, catching one straining nipple in the heat of his mouth and suckling hard, nipping gently at the delicate skin and creating a stinging pleasure that took her right over the edge in an instant. The world disappeared, as she was whirled into a blazing oblivion, seeing nothing, hearing nothing, only *feeling,* feeling at the highest, wildest pinnacle of sensation that she had ever known.

Somewhere in the back of her mind she registered the harsh, primitive cry that told her that Andreas was with her in the most intimate way possible and she felt his hard body clench and tighten as he followed her out of reality and into the scorching ecstasy that had claimed them both.

For a long, long time they lay there, mindless, sightless, breathless, Andreas' wide chest heaving as he struggled to come back to reality. And only then did Becca dare to do what she most wanted as she folded her arms around his big, still shuddering body, feeling the aftershocks of pleasure pulsing through him as she held him close. Her heart clenched with bitter-sweet delight as, barely conscious, he turned his head and pressed the sweetest, most tender kiss on her cheek before he tumbled into sleep. And a moment later she followed him, still holding him in her arms.

She had no idea how long she lay there, blissfully unconscious, she only knew that at last, slowly and reluctantly, she
swam up from the dark waters of sleep and into the real world
again to find that beyond the bedroom window the sun was
already beginning to set. The brightness of the afternoon was
fading, and darkening shadows were starting to fill the room.
But they were as nothing when compared with the shadows
that were creeping into her mind and heart.

Beside her, Andreas still slept deeply, his head pillowed on
her arm, jet-black hair fallen forward over his wide brow, his
strong jaw starting to be darkened by a day's growth of
stubble. His breathing was deep and even and, encouraged by
the fact that he was so dead to the world and so had no idea
of what she was doing, she allowed herself just to lie there
and watch him, studying his sleeping face—his sleeping,
beloved face—so intently that it seemed as if she needed to
imprint its image on her mind, store it up there like supplies
hoarded carefully against a future famine.

And she might truly have to do that, Becca admitted to herself,
acknowledging with a desperate, sinking sensation of sadness
that after this there was no way things could ever be the same.

Sighing deeply, she lay on her back and stared up at the
white-painted ceiling above her, with eyes that fear and misery
made blind, the bitter tears stinging hard, fighting to fall.

'We can't go back,' she whispered to herself, recalling how
on the way upstairs she had been thinking how this one special
time with the man she loved could be so extraordinary, so new,
so fresh, so wonderful in a way that it could never be again.

Even if Andreas' memory never returned, there was no
way they could repeat that exceptional, unique and magical
moment of finding each other again in a way that almost
matched—and totally outclassed—the time that she had lost

her virginity to Andreas, just a few weeks after they had met. That glorious time had gone for good and things could never be as great as that again.

And the cold, creeping sensation of fear that ate into her heart forced her to face the truth and to acknowledge the worry that things could only go downhill from here.

Downhill to where? How far could things go? How bad could it be?

Beside her, Andreas stirred, muttering faintly in his sleep, the sound drawing her head round sharply to look into his face just as he stretched lazily and opened his eyes, his black gaze looking straight into her clouded blue one.

And what she saw in those dark depths made Becca's blood run icy cold in her veins as she realised that things could very definitely get a whole lot worse.

And they just had.

# CHAPTER NINE

ANDREAS had been dreaming.

Deep in sleep, he had been in a world that was so very different from the hot sunny day he had known when he was awake. A cooler, greyer world, but one where his most vivid impression was of green—lush green grass, rich and smooth as velvet, that sprang under his feet as he walked towards the huge marquee tent that was set up right in the middle of the vast lawn.

Inside the tent there was the buzz of conversation, the clatter of glasses and every now and then a ripple of laughter. And his eyes, the blurred eyes he had in his dream, were assailed by the sight of hundreds of people, all crowded together. To his unfocused sight, the men were just grey or black blurs, the women multicoloured, bright and silky, so brilliant they made his head ache.

He didn't know what he was doing here. Didn't feel that he belonged. He only knew that this was where he had to be—that they all seemed to be expecting him, because they turned when he came in, all those faceless people, turned and lifted their glasses in a toast, cheering and saying, 'Congratulations, Andreas! Congratulations!'

To Andreas' horror the words felt almost like physical

scrapes against his skin, ripping away some much-needed protective layer and leaving him raw and disturbingly sensitive. They added to his sense of being in the wrong place, at the wrong time, with the wrong people. There was no one there he could recognise, no one he could turn to, to start a conversation with or even risk giving a smile.

Not that he wanted to smile at anyone. His mood was quite the wrong one for this happy, cheery gathering too. He felt more like a wild, hungry, savage wolf that had prowled into a gathering of birds of paradise and was hunting for just the right one to pounce upon, to tear to shreds with the teeth that were clenched tight inside his aching jaw. He knew just which one he was looking for, and he stalked amongst the happy party, struggling to control the ferocious snarl that threatened to escape him at any moment. She was there somewhere—instinctively he knew that his prey was female—she was there, and when he found her…

Suddenly the room fell silent. The buzzing, chattering, brilliant birds of paradise stopped moving, stopped talking, became totally still. And over at the far side of the marquee he could see her. Tall and slender—and totally in white… plain, simple, unadorned white from head to toe, in stark contrast to the colours all around him. When he saw her his tense jaw fell open for a moment as he snatched in a breath, then his teeth came together with a snap as he turned, headed straight for her. The crowd parted to let him through, a wide, clear path was opening up, taking him straight to her.

He couldn't see her face, not even the blur of pink that was everyone else. She was *white*. Nothing but white. Did she even have a face?

And then, as he came nearer, nearer, suddenly he could hear a single voice, a young, female voice, loud and clear and bubbling with contained laughter, barely held back.

'I do—I do—I do!'

'I do—I do—I do…'

The words repeated over and over in his head until his thoughts swam with the force of it.

'I do—I do—I do…'

And behind him the crowd murmured and laughed and broke into spontaneous applause. Applause that swung around and over the words, breaking into them but never quite drowning them out.

'I do—I do—I do…'

His head was aching from it, the pressure at his temples unendurable. He wanted to lift his hands and rub at them to ease the pressure but he found he couldn't do so. Something had them trapped, tying them down, keeping them from moving. He heard another voice groan aloud and realised with a violent shock to his system that it was his, and that the words he had been trying to form were the same as those in the laughing voice inside his head.

I do.

I *do*!

Rough and unclear, they were enough to make the white-clad figure before him turn sharply. Blinking hard, he found that his gaze would focus more, his vision sharpening just a little. She was wearing a veil, he realised. A long white, flowing veil that hid her face, concealing it completely. But when she saw him she smiled. He couldn't see the smile but he knew it was there. He could sense it with some primitive instinct that came to him with the dream. He knew that she smiled in the same way that he knew he didn't like the smile one little bit.

'Andreas…' she said and her voice was low, huskily seductive.

And then she threw back her veil and all he could see were her eyes—her amazing, pale blue eyes—sea-coloured eyes…

And in his head all that he could hear was that laughter-filled voice saying yet again, 'Oh, I do—I do—I do…'

*Becca*!

The step he took backwards in his dream, the jolt it gave him, brought him awake in rush. Awake to a realisation that the deep green lawn, the marquee, the guests, were all a fantasy. Reality was that he was in his bed, in the villa, that the growing darkness of dusk was gathering round…

And that he was not alone.

He smelled her skin before he opened his eyes, inhaled the warm, intensely personal fragrance of her body, heard the soft sound of her breathing, and knew that some woman shared his bed. The scent of passion, too, was on the sheets, a wild intensity of sex, the after-effects of which still lingered in the heaviness of his limbs, the feeling of deep fulfilment, the strong reluctance to move at all. But at the same time some-thing was nagging at his thoughts, taking him back into his dream for a moment and then out again, back into the present. Something that warned him he had to wake up, had to think, had to act.

With an effort he forced his heavy eyelids open and found himself looking straight into those same beautiful sea-coloured eyes. The eyes of the woman in his dream. Eyes that were watching him with a look of wary apprehension in their smoky depths.

And the taste of betrayal was terrible and sour in his mouth.

'*Rebecca*!'

No one said her name quite like Andreas, Becca reflected privately. No one else put quite that exotic intonation onto the syllables, making it sound like a totally different word. And no one else had ever put such an icy tone into his use of her name, a freezing fury that made her feel as if she had suddenly stepped onto the most dangerous black ice.

'My darling wife—what the hell are you doing here?'

'I—should have thought that that was obvious.'

She regretted the words the minute she had spoken them. Regretted the stupid attempt at flippancy in her tone, the even rasher gesture of her hand that indicated the rumpled bed on which they lay, the disorder of the sheets, the crumpled pillows. It also, to her deep mortification, drew attention to her naked state, brought those frozen black eyes to skim over her body, seeming to sear the delicate skin as they went so that hot colour flooded her cheeks and in a moment of pure embarrassment she reached desperately for the nearest sheet.

'I think it's a little late for that now,' Andreas drawled in cynical contempt. 'Now that I remember my past, I have no recollection of immediate events…so….'

His eyes narrowed, his tone darkening.

'Are you going to tell me just what happened here?'

'You know what happened!'

He did—didn't he? Andreas had recognised her; he had called her his wife with that appallingly savage note in his voice. Somehow, something that had happened had jarred loose whatever had been blocking his memory and while he was asleep the scattered jigsaw pieces had been falling into place. But how complete was it? Did he remember *everything*?

And what picture did the completed jigsaw show?

'We—we made…'

'We had sex,' Andreas interrupted harshly as she stumbled over the words, unable to say 'made love' when confronted by his darkly scowling face, the contempt that blazed in the jet-black eyes. 'That much is obvious. What I mean is just what are you doing here in the first place? I told you to get out and stay out.'

'I know you did—but I—couldn't.'

'And why not? Don't tell me that you've come back to say you're sorry—that—'

'Of course not!'

Becca's total rejection of his challenge rang in her voice. How could he think that *she* had anything to apologise for? Andreas was the one who had declared to her face that he had only married her for sex.

'I thought not.'

Andreas flung himself off the bed and stalked across the room to where the black swimming shorts he had discarded with such eagerness—and her willing help—such a short time before lay in a crumpled heap on the floor. Snatching them up, he pulled them on, every rough, brusque movement speaking of hostility and aggression without a word needing to be spoken.

'Much as I love the image of you curled up in my bed with only a sheet to cover you, I think I would prefer it if you put some clothes on,' he flung into Becca's ashen face. 'I'd like to have this conversation without any unnecessary—distractions.'

'I can't.'

Becca couldn't allow her thoughts to dwell on the idea that the sight of her naked body could still 'distract' Andreas. It wasn't the effect she wanted to have on him. Or was it? Her body still sang from the sensual effect of his lovemaking—his attentions, she amended painfully. Her blood was still hot, her skin prickling with sensitivity so that just the feel of the finest cotton of the sheets against it was almost too much to bear. Her body ached in places, there were tiny bruised spots in others, but they were aches and bruises she didn't mind at all.

Her nipples were still tender, and the intimate spots between her legs still pulsed faintly with the aftershocks of passion. The thought of having to pull on the close-fitting Lycra swimsuit was frankly unbearable.

'The only thing I have to wear in here is that…'

An unwary wave of her arm towards where the lavender swimming costume lay in a similar state to his shorts let the sheet slip and she snatched it up again, clutching it to her as if it was a shield against those black, accusing eyes. She saw Andreas' mouth twitch in an almost-smile of the darkest humour, and shivered when she realised how bleak and stony his eyes remained, no light in them at all.

'In that case I prefer the sheet.'

No, he didn't, Andreas told himself reprovingly. The sheet was almost as bad as nothing at all. The fine cotton lay lightly over the slender lines of her body, clinging to the curves of her hips, the rise and fall of her breasts, defining them in a way that made his throat dry. And even beneath the white material, the faint dark shadow between her thighs was visible, reminding him of the way those curls had felt against the most intimate, most sensual parts of his body. Just recalling it made the roar of blood thunder in his head so that he could barely think straight.

OK, admit it, he told himself, you don't want to think at all. What he wanted was to throw himself down on the bed beside her, rip the sheet from her body and start to make love to her all over again. The taste of her lips, of her breasts was still in his mouth, her scent was on his skin, blending with his own into the most intoxicating perfume he had ever inhaled. It went straight to his head like the most potent *ouzo*, clouding it and making it spin.

When combined with the heat of pounding lust, it was a

brutally lethal combination, making him feel as if his head was a volcano where red-hot lava was just pushing to the top, waiting to explode.

No. He needed to keep a grip on himself, on his temper. He had to think clearly. His body, his senses, might be thrilled to see Becca again but common sense warned him to tread very carefully. If she was back then it was for her own purposes, and he wanted to know just what they were before he made a foolish move.

*Another* foolish move. She'd already got under his guard once, while his brain was scrambled from the accident. He wasn't going to let that happen again.

But just the sight of her made him so damn sexually hungry. After living for almost a year without her, he might have thought that he had forgotten the impact she had on his senses. But it seemed that she had only to walk back into his life and he was a slave to his libido like some horny adolescent in the throes of his first physical affair.

He might have thought that he'd have forgotten… *Hah*!

A harshly cynical laugh broke from him as he realised the bitter irony of what he had just thought. He'd spent the last months trying to force himself to forget that someone called Becca Ainsworth—Becca Petrakos legally, but very definitely not morally—had ever existed.

And failed miserably.

'Andreas?'

Becca was watching him—nervously, he could almost swear. He had never realised that she was such a good actress. But sitting there like that, with the sheet twisted tightly round her, those beautiful blue eyes wide in a damnably perfect face, she looked the picture of innocence. So innocent that he could almost believe in her himself.

This was the Becca he'd tried to push from his mind. But then the accident had done that for him by wiping her from his memory, and in the time that he had been out of it she had walked back in, cool as could be. And lied through her teeth to him.

And he had been fool enough to let his lust for her drown out all thought of common sense. One tug on the golden chain of sensuality that tied them both together and he had fallen straight into bed with her. Right where she wanted him, it seemed.

But why? What did she want from him? Not just sex, that was obvious. She had to have something else up her sleeve.

So what had happened between her and her precious Roy Stanton? Because something must have done to bring her here, like this, when she had vowed that she would rather die than come back.

'On second thoughts…'

He turned towards the door, where his black towelling robe hung. Grabbing it, he tossed it roughly in Becca's direction, not caring that it overshot by several metres and landed on the floor on the other side of the bed.

'Put that on. I've had enough of the sight of you.'

Liar, his conscience reproached him. Hadn't today—the past couple of days—taught him anything? He could never get enough of the sight of her, the feel of her, the taste of her. He doubted if he ever would. The truth was that passion made him a fool where Becca was concerned and that was a feeling he didn't like one little bit.

'And then we talk. You can start explaining just what the hell you are up to.'

'I'm not "up to" anything!' Becca protested, struggling to get off the bed and reach the black robe, while at the same time keeping the sheet securely wrapped around her.

'No?'

'No!'

'It seems that way to me. You surely don't expect me to believe that you turned up here out of love for me—to beg me to take you back? No—I thought not,' he added when he saw the way her face changed, her lips pinching tight together. 'So you've obviously come for something, and I want to know what.'

And when he did know he would take a great delight in throwing his rejection of her request right back in her face, Becca told herself as she tried once more to grab the black robe. She'd really messed up this time. What had possessed her to fall into bed with him like that, forgetting all about the reasons why she was here? She should have known that there was a chance that something like passionate lovemaking—passionate *sex,* she amended painfully—together with the fact that she'd been wearing the lavender costume that had practically been the last thing he'd seen her in, would be likely to stir his memories, if not actually bring them right back. She would never be able to forgive herself if she threw away Daisy's chance of the life-saving operation because of her own foolish passion.

She had the robe in her hand now, but when it came to pulling it on, while still holding on to the sheet that was wrapped round her, she found the situation was impossible. And it was made all the worse by the fact that Andreas stood, dark and devastating, on the far side of the room, watching her through cynically amused black eyes.

'You might have the courtesy to look away,' she flung at him in indignation, knowing that the struggle she was having was making her face look pink and flustered.

'Why?' he shot back, leaning against the wall and folding his arms across his chest as he met her furious glare with icy calm. 'Did you do that for me? Did you look away when I got out of bed—or before that? Did you insist on covering your own eyes then?'

'That's different.'

'Is it? Then will you please tell me how? I'd like to know why it's fine for you to ogle me when I'm naked but not for me—'

'I did not *ogle*!' she flashed furiously.

'Seemed that way to me. I could almost feel your hot little eyes on me all the way across the room. But then I am not so much of a hypocrite as to pretend to a rush of false modesty so soon after I have been—what is it you say?—rolling around in the sack just a short time before.'

'It's not a pretence! I—I don't feel right that way. Not any more.'

'Not any more,' Andreas echoed darkly and the cynicism of his tone made her tense instinctively, waiting for the brutal lash of his tongue in quick response.

To her surprise it didn't come. Instead, Andreas' face closed up, setting hard and cold until it looked as if his features were carved from granite, his eyes just polished jet.

'My apologies,' he declared in a tone that made a mockery of the polite words. 'In that case, I will wait for you downstairs. I think we would both feel more capable of holding this discussion on more neutral territory. I'll make us some coffee—you'll be…what? Five minutes?'

That 'five minutes' was an order, not a suggestion, and, leaving Becca still fighting to find a way to respond that didn't make her look petty or weak, he turned on his heel and walked out.

She could almost hear the steady ticking of some imaginary stopwatch as she listened to his footsteps going down the landing.

# CHAPTER TEN

SHE made it downstairs in seven minutes.

She had been determined not to let Andreas think that he could just click his fingers and she would jump to do as he said. But all the same, stirring it too much by keeping him waiting deliberately was not a clever idea. His temper would only darken by the minute and, as he had already started out with it almost as black as it could be, she didn't want to take unnecessary risks.

First she had had to go to her own room to find her clothes and snatch a quick shower. The extra seconds had ticked away while she had dithered over what to wear.

Just what did one wear to a sort of emotional trial? she wondered on a wave of near-hysteria. A trial in which Andreas was not only judge and jury but also very definitely counsel for the prosecution all at once. The lightweight sun-dress that was her first choice was discarded as being too revealing and frivolous. A white T-shirt and Indian print skirt went the same way when the button on the waistband of the skirt proved suddenly to be somehow too complicated for her unsteady fingers to fasten easily.

In the end she had kept the T-shirt and pulled on denim

jeans to go with it before deciding that enough was enough—
she'd made her point without risking him actually losing it
completely—and hurrying down the stairs after him.

Andreas was in the big sitting room that opened onto the
pool area. The first thing that Becca noticed about him was
that he too had taken a moment to dress and was now wearing
a short-sleeved black shirt, hanging open over his tanned
chest, and loose black linen trousers that hung low on his
narrow hips. Like her, he was barefooted, as he so often was
around the house.

He had opened the patio doors and was standing gazing out
at the glorious view of the ocean, but Becca had the distinct
impression that he didn't see anything but was intent on his
own thoughts. He had a mug of the strong black coffee he in-
variably drank in one hand, and another mug containing a less
potent version of the drink stood on the coffee-table behind
him. He didn't turn when Becca arrived, or make any sign of
having noticed that she was there, but continued to stare,
frowning, at the horizon until, after waiting a few moments
to see what he would do, she cleared her throat pointedly.

'You wanted to talk to me.'

His turn was slow, deliberately so, she felt and when he was
facing her he let those deep-set black eyes run over her from
the top of her head, still wet from her shower, down to her feet,
and back up again.

'*Déjà vu,*' he murmured on a note of irony. 'Haven't we
been here before?'

It was only then that Becca realised that they were in fact
both dressed as if for a replay of the dreadful scene on the
evening of their wedding day. The scene that had ended their
marriage. The recollection was enough to drain some of the
hard-won strength from her legs and make her think twice

about picking up the mug of coffee for fear that her hand would shake so badly it would give away the way her nerves were tying themselves into tight, uncomfortable knots in her stomach. Instead she perched on the arm of one of the big leather-covered settees, hoping she looked moderately at ease.

'So what are we going to talk about?'

Andreas took a sip from his coffee, stared down into the mug as if looking for inspiration in the dark liquid. The movement made Becca realise that, like her, he had snatched the time to have a fast shower before coming downstairs, his hair was still soaking too. But, unlike hers, the wet look flattered him, giving the blue-black strands a glistening sheen and a slightly spiky look that suited him, while her own heavily flattened, sodden rats' tails had quite the opposite effect.

'Why don't we start with you telling me just what was so important to you that you were prepared to sell yourself to get it?'

Becca was glad that she was sitting down. She felt sure that her legs would have gone from under her if she hadn't, with the cutting force of his attack. But even though she was sitting, she still clung onto the back of the settee for extra support.

'I didn't—I wasn't—I *didn't*!'

'Oh, so what are you claiming—that you didn't have sex with me just now, in that bed…?'

An arrogant tilt of his dark head in the direction of the ceiling and so the bedroom above them emphasised his point.

'I—you know I did.'

Did he have to keep saying 'have sex' in that brutal way? It reminded her too painfully of his cold-blooded declaration that he had married her for sex and nothing more.

'So you must have wanted to use that sex to get something from me.'

'No! No way! I never—I wouldn't…'

'Wouldn't you? Well, you do surprise me. So that leaves only one other possible alternative, and I have to say that I really never thought that you'd admit to that.'

'I'm not admitting to anything,' Becca growled. 'And what is the only other possible alternative?'

Andreas flashed her a wide, deceptively innocent look from huge, brilliant jet-black eyes.

'Why, the fact that you were so overcome with need—with passion for me—that you just couldn't help yourself. That nothing else in the world mattered but that we should come together in bed…'

'It wasn't that!'

'No? Then—to go back to my original interpretation of your actions—you *were* using sex to get something from me.'

'I wasn't—no! I didn't!'

'Oh, please, Rebecca!' Andreas exclaimed in exasperation. Coming to the table, he slammed his mug down on it with such force that some of the coffee slopped over the side.

'Credit me with a little intelligence. It's either one thing or the other. What other possible explanation could there be?'

The fact that she was head over heels in love with him, crazy about him in a way that made her a fool to herself, weakened all her defences and left her totally vulnerable where he was concerned. That she hadn't been able to say no to the thought of being with him just one last time.

'A mad moment?' she said flippantly, trying desperately to distract him from the way that he was thinking. 'After all, we were always good—great together that way. You said it yourself—no one ever made you as hot as I do.'

The way his black brows drew together in a dark frown alerted her to the fact that she'd said something he didn't like. And she winced inwardly as she realised just what it was.

He'd flung those exact words at her in the appalling row on the day of their marriage, destroying all her hopes and dreams in one blow.

*I married you for sex—for that and nothing else. No other woman has ever made me feel as hot as you do.*

'A mad moment, hmm…'

He had come too close. If she was not careful, then surely he would see the truth in her face, read it at the backs of her eyes.

'Mad, certainly, but not totally crazy.'

Andreas flung himself down into the chair opposite and sprawled back against the cushions, long legs stretched out in front of him, crossed at the ankles, elbows resting on the chair arms, long fingers steepled together under his chin.

'Which is what you'd have to be to have come here just for that.'

His brilliant black gaze seemed to sear into her skull, trying to pull out the truth whether she was prepared to give it to him or not.

'My, you do think a lot of yourself, don't you?' Becca used defiance to try to hide the way she was really feeling. 'Do you really think that I'd travel all this way just for a quick tumble into bed with you?'

'No.'

Andreas' wickedly slow smile told her how easily she had fallen into the trap he had dug right at her feet.

'I really do not think that—which is why I keep asking the question that you seem to want to go to any lengths possible to avoid. You're not drinking your coffee,' he added in a way that sounded like an afterthought but which left Becca very much afraid that he knew exactly *why* she wasn't drinking.

'I don't fancy it.'

'The coffee or telling me why you're here?'

'Either, if you must know!'

She really had to stop trying to be flippant. It was getting her nowhere and was obviously starting to rile him. The way that he compressed his lips into a thin, hard line told her that he was fighting to hold back the sort of acid retort that would be capable of flaying half the skin from her ears just to hear it.

'So what is it you have to hide?'

'Nothing—it's just…'

'Rebecca!' Andreas' tone was low, almost soft, but it was the softness of the hiss of a hooded python, just before it struck with deadly force, and it made Becca flinch inwardly simply to hear it. 'Tell me…tell me now why you are here or pack your bags and get out of my life—and this time make it for good.'

If she did that then she would never be able to help Daisy—and she would never be able to see him ever again. Right now, Becca couldn't begin to think which of those two possibilities hurt most. But then the truth was that when her heart was one mass of pain, how could she tell if any one particular spot was worse than any other?

'Can't you guess?' she muttered, low and uneven.

'I want you to tell me,' Andreas returned, face rigid, expression unyielding.

'Isn't it obvious?' she no longer cared if she sounded desperate; it was how she felt. 'You always said I'd come back for money and—well, here I am.'

'You came for money?' He actually sounded—what? He couldn't be disappointed but that was the note that was in his voice.

'Don't sound so surprised, Andreas—you always knew this would happen! You should have made that bet you wanted—the one where you said that I'd come looking for cash before the year was up. Because you'd have been right. Here I am and it's money I'm after.'

It was the only way she could get it out. She couldn't go on her knees and beg. And for some reason she couldn't bring herself to talk about Daisy—not yet. She didn't feel strong enough, brave enough, to open herself up to him like that. Not after all that had happened and the brutal damage he had inflicted on her heart. So she'd gone on to the attack, wanting to lash out, repay hurt with hurt.

'Money for what?'

'Does it matter?'

'To me it does.'

'But you've been proved right. That should give you immense satisfaction. I've shown myself to be the greedy—'

'It gives me no satisfaction,' Andreas cut in, cold and flat. 'No satisfaction at all. If you want the truth I would rather you had stayed away for ever than that you turned up here like this—for this.'

How the hell could anyone think it would give him satisfaction to be proved right like this? He had once loved this woman, once wanted her to be in his life for ever—and she had betrayed him even before the vows had been spoken.

Wasn't that what his dream had been about? About the way that he had had warning of what she was really like and yet had gone ahead with their wedding all the same. He had wanted to believe in her, to trust her, to put his faith in the one woman he had ever loved with all his heart. And so because he had loved her he had married her, convinced that the terrible things he had heard about her were lies.

And found out that they were the truth.

Did she think that he really would enjoy going through that hell all over again?

'So tell me—what is it for? Have you gambled yourself into ruin? Spent a fortune you don't possess? Developed an appalling cocaine habit?'

'I would never do that!' Becca protested, looking horrified that he would even consider it. 'No, none of those.'

At least that was some sort of a relief. But it still left the other, less endurable reason why she might want the money.

'Then why do you want the money so badly? Who do you want it for?'

'Who?'

Becca's head came up and she stared into his face with obvious confusion clouding her eyes.

'Who would I—?'

'Let me make it plain so you have no chance of mis-understanding: tell me that this money is not for him—not for Roy Stanton.'

'Roy…no—no, it's not!'

It was almost convincing but he had seen the way that her eyes had dropped, just for a split-second, her sea-coloured gaze sliding away as she gathered herself, thought hastily and then nerved herself to face him again.

'It's not for him.'

Andreas couldn't sit there any longer looking into her beautiful face, into those wide, brilliant eyes, and know she wasn't telling the truth. He couldn't stand to watch those soft, full lips frame the lies that made his disgust a fury of rage inside his head.

He didn't want to remember the number of times he had kissed those lips, all unknowing of the lies that had come to them so easily. He didn't want to be tempted by the fact that all he had to do was lean forward, take that sexy body into his arms, press his mouth to hers, and in the fiery explosion of sensuality that was sure to follow they would both forget about the reasons why she was here, the past and all that had come between them.

If only he hadn't taken her to bed this afternoon so that the memory of the passion that could flare between them at a touch was now so fresh in his mind. He only had to look at her and his body ached with need; he was hot and hard just thinking of her. His hands yearned to touch, his lips to kiss, every one of his senses clamoured for appeasement of its hunger. He had tried telling himself that she was not as gorgeous as he remembered, but taking her again after so long had only made him realise how wrong he had been. Once had not been enough—it could never be enough. All it had done was to serve to make him realise how much he wanted her again and again, more than ever before.

The satisfaction he had known in her bed this afternoon had totally evaporated already. It had only been enough to show him that he could never, ever sate himself on this woman, if he was to spend a lifetime trying.

'Tell the truth, damn you!' The hungry demands of his body made his words harsher and rougher than before.

Flinging himself to his feet, he made himself move across the room, putting as much distance between himself and Becca as possible, pushing his hands deep into the pockets of his trousers to conceal the way they had clenched into tight, angry fists.

'Don't lie to me, Rebecca! Never lie to me—not if you want to have any hope of getting what you want.'

'I'm not lying.'

'You are if you tell me that Stanton has nothing to do with this.'

That got through to her. Her face went white, all colour deserting her cheeks, and her mouth fell open in shock. So he'd been right in his suspicions. It didn't make him feel any better to know it. Instead, he felt sick with contempt.

'I'll ask you again—does Stanton have anything to do with the reason why you want this money?'

How did she answer that? Becca thought miserably. Because she knew that just mentioning the name Roy Stanton was like setting a match to paper-dry tinder where Andreas was concerned, and she'd tried to dodge the truth once—not actually lying but avoiding answering with strict veracity as far as she could. Now that he'd changed the question, there was no hope she could do that again.

'Don't bother to say anything, Rebecca.'

She'd hesitated too long and Andreas had jumped to the inevitable conclusion.

'I can see your answer in your face.'

She would have sworn that it was impossible for Andreas' face to close up any tighter, his eyes to get any colder, or his expression any more distant, but somehow he had managed it.

'I think you've had a wasted journey, Rebecca. You should have stayed at home and spared yourself the effort of coming all this way for nothing. You might have thought that deceiving me into believing that you had come to look after me so that you could worm your way into my bed would enslave me sexually again so that I could deny you nothing—'

'It wasn't like that!' Becca protested sharply, but Andreas continued without pausing, speaking over her as if she had never tried to say a thing.

'Unfortunately for you, I got my memory back before you could really work on me, but I think you should know that you were foolish even to try. I don't put my head into that sort of noose twice.'

'I didn't…' Becca tried, but Andreas shook his head, his refusal to listen stamped into every line on his face.

'If you're wise, you'll leave it there, Rebecca. You will only make things so much worse if you continue.'

Pulling his hands out of his pockets, where they had been pushed deep all this time, he raked both of them through the black silk of his hair, ruffling it wildly, and Becca bit down hard on her lower lip as a sudden yearning desire to go and smooth it down for him caught her painfully on the raw.

Then he was speaking again, heading for the open patio doors as he did so.

'I threw you out of my life once because of him, and I'm quite prepared to do it all over again. In fact, I would prefer it if you left now. I'm going for a walk on the beach—and I don't want to find you here when I get back.'

'Andreas…' Becca tried but she was talking to his back. He was moving so fast, with such ruthless determination, that he was already outside, already heading away from her physically when he had been so distant from her mentally all the time.

She couldn't let him go. Not like this. If she did then any hope of saving baby Daisy were gone for good, and she would rather die than let that happen. She had to try and get him to reconsider.

'Andreas—please…'

But he continued walking, not even glancing round at her. His long, straight back was held so stiffly upright, his proud head so high, that she could almost see her words bouncing off the invisible walls of defence that he had built around himself.

'Andreas—don't…'

She stepped out after him into the heat of the sunny afternoon.

'The money's not for me—or for—for him…'

She didn't dare to actually speak Roy Stanton's name, knowing the incendiary effect it had on Andreas.

· 'It's for a child—a baby...'

He'd stopped at least. But she still had to get him to turn round. Right now he could still walk on—away from her.

'Please listen.'

He was turning. Slowly—but he was turning to face her. Her heart leapt with relief, leaving her breathless and shaky.

'A baby?'

He managed to inject the words with such scepticism, such disbelief that she fully expected him to fling a rejection in her face and move on. She had his attention for now; she had to hold on to it and make him understand.

'A little girl—Daisy—she's desperately sick and—'

'*Whose* baby?'

It slashed through her words as she struggled to get them out. And at the same time those blazing black eyes seared over her from top to toe, taking in her slender figure, lingering on her waist...

'No, not mine,' she hastened to assure him. 'Daisy's not my baby—though I love her as if she were. She—she's my niece. And I would do anything I could to help her.'

'Niece?' Andreas echoed as if he did not understand the word. '*Anepsia*? You do not have a niece.'

'Yes, I do—she's my sister's little girl. And before you say that I don't have a sister,' Becca rushed on when he opened his mouth, clearly planning to do just that, 'let me tell you that I do. A half-sister, that is. But I didn't know about her for years. I only found out about her—quite recently.'

She paused, waiting for Andreas to ask the next question, but he remained silent, hands on narrow hips, black eyes fixed on her face, obviously waiting for her to go on.

'You know that I'm adopted. That I was born when my biological mother was only sixteen? And my mum and dad adopted me as a tiny baby. I told you…' she prompted, needing some response from him before she could go on. She couldn't just pour the whole story out while he stood there, silent and withdrawn, as distant from her as if some huge cavern had opened up on the stone-flagged terrace, separating them from each other.

A faint, brief inclination of his dark head was all the acknowledgement Andreas made and then he was still again, obviously waiting for her to continue.

'I've been trying to find my birth mother—to see if I had any family. Blood family. I thought it was important to know.'

She couldn't tell him that this search had taken on a whole new meaning and importance from the moment that Andreas had asked her to marry him. That she had really felt the need to know about her family then, to know if she had some blood ties, someone who was linked to her that way. And deep down there had also been a secret, private need to know if there were any health problems she needed to take into consideration if she and Andreas were ever to have children. That was one concern that no longer mattered at all, she told herself miserably.

'I found that my mother was dead—and she'd never known who my father was. But I had a half-sister—Macy. I managed to get in touch with her—meet her.'

'And when was this?'

Becca bit her lip in discomfort. She'd known this question would come, but being prepared for it didn't make it easy to answer.

'Just before our wedding.'

'I see.'

Andreas took a step backwards, and the arms that had been at his sides were now crossed over his broad chest. He couldn't have put a distance between them more effectively if he'd tried.

'And you didn't think to tell me?'

'I—couldn't. Macy had—some problems and she made me promise not to tell anyone.'

Once, perhaps, she might have explained all this in detail to him. Once he would have been owed the full story. But Macy had been so insistent that no one should know. If she'd breathed a word, she would have lost the sister she'd just found. Macy had only just discovered about Daisy then. And the realisation that there was a baby on the way had made everything so much more urgent; made it so much more important that she stay in touch with her half-sister, and with the baby who was to become her darling niece.

And then Andreas had forfeited the right to know anything more about her when he had declared that he had never loved her and their marriage was only for sex before throwing her out of the house.

'I would have told my husband as soon as I could—but then you weren't my husband long enough for that to matter at all.'

Andreas actually flinched as the barb she flung at him went home, and just for a moment some emotion that she didn't understand flashed across his face. It was there and gone again before she had time to even try to interpret it and the stone-wall look was fully back in place again.

'So Macy is the mother of this Daisy?'

'Yes. And Daisy's just eleven weeks old—'

'And who is the father?'

The words seemed unnaturally loud in the silence of the sunny garden. The inevitable question. The obvious question. And one she would dodge if she could. She desperately wished that she could.

'Does it matter?' she hedged nervously, knowing as soon as she heard it that her voice gave her away, the way it broke in the middle, making it obvious that she had something to hide.

'The look on your face tells me that it does,' Andreas told her harshly, his tone as cold as ice. 'So tell me—who is the father of this baby?'

Becca's jaw seemed to have frozen stiff so that it was impossible to open her mouth to answer him, even if she had wanted to. And she didn't want to. Every time she tried to force herself to speak, she looked into Andreas' dark, shuttered face and a terrible sense of dread overwhelmed her. Bitter tears stung at the backs of her eyes and she blinked hard, trying to force them back. But she knew why they were there. Fear had put them there. Fear of what would happen as soon as she spoke.

She feared it for poor baby Daisy, who needed this man to help her so much—and yet who would probably be condemned not for anything she had done but for the simple biological fact of who her father was.

And she feared it for herself because she dreaded how she was going to feel if Andreas did reject her and walk away in a black, unforgiving fury as soon as she spoke the name that enraged him so much.

And she knew that he wouldn't let go of this until he knew.

'Becca...' Andreas' use of her name was a warning, but it was the fact that he had once more reverted to the shorter, more affectionate form of it that finished her completely. The tears she had struggled against wouldn't be held back any longer but flooded her eyes and a single one spilled out and ran slowly down her cheek.

'Don't ask me...' she whispered, and to her astonishment Andreas accepted her plea and didn't push her any more. But only because he didn't need to. Her response, the distress she couldn't hide, had given him her answer.

'Roy Stanton,' he declared, hard and flat. 'The baby's father is Roy Stanton.'

It was a statement, not a question, but still Becca had to give him an answer, though all she could do was nod silently, the ability to speak having deserted her completely.

'Roy Stanton,' Andreas repeated, the other man's name almost like a curse on his lips.

She couldn't read his expression through the blur of tears but she didn't have to. All she needed to know about his reaction was there in his voice, in the way he spat out the words.

And then it was as she had always dreaded it would be when, without another word, Andreas turned on his heel and walked away from her, striding fast and determinedly over the terrace and down the roughly carved steps that led from the cliff to the shore. Rejection and hostility were stamped into every line of his powerful body and she knew that if she tried to call him back he would refuse to even show that he had heard.

And besides, she couldn't find the strength to do so. She didn't know what she could say to change his mind, and even if she'd been able to think of anything her voice wouldn't work. So all she could do was stand and watch through tear-drenched eyes, staring after him until he disappeared from view.

# CHAPTER ELEVEN

DOWN in the bay, a lively breeze was whipping up the sea into unruly waves. The water whirled and swayed, rising up into foam-topped peaks and then hurling itself against the shore in a swirling rush before ebbing back out again fast, in a way that had it sucking at the sand, drawing it back with it.

The atmosphere suited Andreas' mood perfectly. The restless movement all about him was in keeping with his own frame of mind, the way that he couldn't make his thoughts settle into any balanced pattern. Instead they swung from burning rage to icy cold and back again in every second that passed.

*Roy Stanton.*

He kicked viciously at the sand as the name burned in his mind, making him clench his teeth hard against the feeling.

*Roy Stanton.*

Almost a year before he had hoped that he had heard the last of that name. That the man who had ruined his life, and taken away the one thing of value he truly loved, was out of his life for ever.

Roy Stanton and Becca between them had destroyed his happiness, and when he had thrown her out of the villa on the evening of their travesty of a wedding day he had hoped—

prayed—that he would never, ever see or hear of either of them again.

And then she had turned up, needing money.

Money for a sick child.

Money for Roy Stanton's sick child.

Standing staring at the sea was doing nothing to ease the restless rage of his thoughts and Andreas set off along the edge of the shore, striding fast, splashing through the water, heedless of the way that the waves broke against his legs, soaking the fine linen of his trousers. He needed the movement to express his feelings, to ease the fury in his mind so that he could think.

There was one thing that stood out clearly. The baby was innocent in all this. How could he not help a sick child? That was not in question. But Roy Stanton…!

Obviously the selfish bastard had moved on from Becca to another woman—*Theos,* he'd moved to her *sister* and had a child by her! And Becca had wept at the thought of it.

Oh, she'd fought with everything that was in her not to show those tears, but he'd seen them sheening her pale eyes, swimming under her lids as she fought to blink them back. Stanton had taken her from him, he'd made her break her wedding vows before she had even spoken the words out loud in the ceremony, and then he had broken her heart by moving on to someone else and fathering a child on her.

And Becca had still come here to plead for help for that baby. Her sister's baby. Her sister's child with her own former lover. His stomach heaved at the thought.

Inevitably, his mind went back to the time just before the wedding. The last time that he had been truly happy. When his future had been like a glorious sun rising out there on the horizon. He was going to be married to the woman he adored.

She was his life and she loved him back—or so he had believed. Another few days, less than a week, and they would be together forever.

And then the phone calls had started.

Foul, sneaking phone calls that spoke of secrets and lies. The voice at the other end of the line had told him that Becca—his fiancée—wasn't the woman he believed her to be. That she didn't love him at all but was only using him; marrying him to get as much money from him as she could. Money that she was then going to share with her real lover...

And for a fee—a substantial fee—he would reveal the name of that lover. For now he would just give the initials. And those initials were RS.

Coming to a halt in his furious march over the sand, Andreas stared out at the horizon with unseeing eyes, shoulders hunched, hands pushed deep into his pockets.

He'd laughed. He'd actually laughed. The story was impossible to believe. He had trusted Becca. There was no way she was deceiving him. He'd slammed the phone down on the call; put it out of his mind.

Until the letter had arrived with a photocopy of a cheque. A cheque for the full amount of the money he had recently given Becca to help her pay for everything she needed for the wedding—right down to the last penny. And the cheque in the copy had been written in his fiancée's handwriting—and made out to one Roy Stanton.

That was when he'd called in an investigator. He'd wanted to get to the bottom of this, find out the truth.

There had been nothing to find, the man he'd hired had assured him. He'd turned up no evidence to link Rebecca Ainsworth to Roy Stanton. The phone calls had been traced to the same Roy Stanton, who was obviously at the back of all this.

Whatever Becca had paid him the money for, he'd obviously wanted more. But Andreas didn't give a damn about the money. He had plenty of that. It was only if the claims that Stanton was Becca's lover were true that he would have acted.

And so he'd put the matter out of his mind and gone through with the wedding. He wouldn't have been human if a doubt, a worry, hadn't flashed across his mind just once— but he pushed them away. One look at his bride's face had been enough to convince him that she was honest, innocent and as much in love with him as he was with her.

It was there in the way that she'd smiled at him, the way she'd looked deep into his eyes when she said her vows. And it had been there in the way that, in reply to the usual question 'Do you take this man…?' she had been unable to hold back in her reply, answering not just with the simple 'I do', but saying:

'Oh, I do—I do—I do…'

At least that was what he had thought. It was what he had wanted to believe too.

He had married the woman he adored; brought her here to his home on this tiny island that his family had owned for centuries, thinking that he could put it all behind him. He'd hardly been able to keep his hands off his beautiful bride, and had made passionate love to her just as soon as they had reached the house. Their marriage couldn't have begun in a more perfect way, he had told himself.

And then the photographs had arrived. The faxes had been waiting for him when he walked into his office. Sent by the investigator he had put on the case. Photos he couldn't deny, no matter how much he wanted to.

Stooping, Andreas picked up a flat stone and flung it into the sea, watching as it skipped its way over several waves, and then sank deep into the water, disappearing without a trace.

Becca hadn't been able to deny anything either, when he'd challenged her with Roy Stanton's name. She'd gone white, and he had seen the near-panic in her eyes. She'd never expected to be found out, that much was obvious. Had she really thought that she could hide her affair with the other man while being married to him?

Had she really thought that the money she could hope to give her lover would keep him by her side?

Because obviously, when she had returned home, her tail between her legs, without the huge financial settlement they must have been expecting, Roy Stanton had grown tired of her and his eye had started wandering. Or perhaps he had wandered even before then, and Becca had been duped all along.

Did she really care for him so much that she would come here, plead for money for his child? Or was the child now her uppermost concern? And if that was why she was here then why—*why*—had she gone to bed with him today?

Just remembering the experience of that afternoon, the passion that had blazed between them, made Andreas' blood pound in his veins, setting his whole body throbbing in recollection. He would pay any price to have that experience all over again.

Any price…

*Daisy's not my baby—though I love her as if she were. She—she's my niece. And I would do anything I could to help her.*

In the back of his thoughts he heard Becca speaking as clearly as if she had been standing behind him, whispering in his ear.

*I would do anything I could to help her.*

All right, let's see if she meant that…

Becca hadn't been able to move from her place on the terrace since Andreas had left her there. She had seemed to be frozen there, her legs unable to move, as she watched him walk away and out of her sight. And then she had sunk down onto one of the low stone walls that edged the terrace, shielding anyone on it from the long, sheer cliff to the sea, covering her eyes with her hands briefly as she faced the fact that she might have ruined everything. That she might have destroyed Daisy's one and only chance of help.

She didn't know how she was going to go back and face Macy, what she was going to tell her sister, if that was true. Macy was barely back on the straight and narrow as it was, and another setback could ruin everything. Brutal claws of anxiety clutched at her heart, making her wish for the relief of tears. But somehow the tears that had burned in her eyes so hotly before, now seemed to have vanished completely, leaving her eyes dry and uncomfortable.

And suddenly she knew why. Whatever had made Andreas walk off like that, it was nothing to do with Daisy. Andreas had been listening, his attention totally focused, when she had been telling him about Macy and her baby. It was only when the name of Roy Stanton had come into the conversation—when he had forced it out of her—that his mood had changed, become blackly savage, and he had turned and walked off without another word. Perhaps there was still hope—and if there was any sort of a chance, she wasn't going to let it go.

She had said that she would do anything she had to to save Daisy's life—and she'd meant it. She only prayed that Andreas would give her the opportunity.

The sun was setting by the time that Andreas came back from the beach. He appeared at the top of the cliff steps just when the burning red ball had hit the horizon, and his tall, powerful figure was silhouetted against it, like some demon appearing out of hell, making Becca shiver in dreadful apprehension in spite of the warmth of the evening.

He had made up his mind, that much was obvious. She could see it in the way he held himself, the tension in his shoulders, the set to his jaw that etched white lines of determination around his nose and mouth. His decision was made, and if he had decided against her then she doubted very much that there was anything she could do to change it for better or worse.

'You're still here,' Andreas said as he came within a few yards of her. It was a statement, not a question, and there was no way of judging his mood from it, or from his tone, so she simply nodded in agreement.

'I was waiting for you,' she said in a low, uncertain voice.

'Why?'

Why? There was an answer for that in her heart, but she had no idea whether she dared to risk giving it to him. But what else did she have?

Taking a deep breath, she forced the words out, fighting to control her voice so that she sounded so much braver than she felt.

'Because I know that no matter what you think of me— or—' her courage failed her at the thought of saying that provocative name '—or Daisy's father, you won't be able to turn your back on a child. You might hate me, but you won't let an innocent baby die if you can help it.'

If her words had been a slap aimed at his face, his head wouldn't have gone back any more sharply. Becca wished she could see his expression but the way he stood with his back to the sun threw his face into shadow and all she could spot was the way that he had closed his eyes just for a moment.

'We need to talk,' was all he said and he walked past her, into the house, not sparing her another glance but obviously expecting her to follow.

Which she did, of course. She had no other option.

In the sitting room, Andreas clicked on a single lamp but that was all. With some light still filling the room from the sinking sun, it was possible to move around, but not to see anything really clearly. But at the same time, the shifting shadows in the room were a sort of comfort, suiting Becca's mood completely. She felt as if she was groping her way forward, hoping that somehow she would end up in the place she most wanted to be.

Though the truth was that right at this moment she had no idea where that might be.

'I could do with a drink,' Andreas said abruptly, making her start in surprise. 'How about you?'

'I—Some wine would be nice,' Becca managed carefully. Perhaps the alcohol would relax her, ease her dry throat, help her handle what she felt was going to be one of the most difficult conversations of her life, second only to the appalling confrontation on the evening of her wedding day.

But that time she had been caught on edge, not knowing what was coming. This time she was desperately tense because she knew exactly what they had to talk about. Right at this moment she had no way of saying which situation was actually worse.

'White or red?'

Did it matter? She knew that he was just preparing the ground, so to speak. He was being polite, offering a drink, settling her down before…

Before what?

That was the really important question. The one she needed answering *now*. But she didn't dare to press the point, to risk pushing Andreas into saying anything he was not ready to say. And so she tried a small smile, almost managed it.

'Red will be fine.'

'I'll get it. I will be back in a moment.'

He was gone much more than a moment. How long did it take to find a bottle, open it—pour? Becca paced around the room like a restless cat, unable to settle, too uneasy to sit still.

Was he ever coming back?

It was as she thought the words that the door opened again and Andreas came back into the room. And at once for Becca it was as if the world had suddenly righted itself again, in a way that had nothing at all to do with the reason why she was here, the question she was waiting for him to answer.

The truth was that she was so desperately in love with this man that simply to be with him, in the same room, so that she could see him, watch him, know he was there, was enough for her. She could see how the burning light from the sunset fell on the raven's-wing darkness of his hair, burnishing it with glowing red tones, look into the blackness of his eyes and see their brilliance in spite of the shadows of the room. She could hear his soft breathing, the pad of his still bare feet on the wooden floor. And the ozone tang of the sea was still on his skin and hair from the time on the beach.

And from wanting things to hurry up, from needing an answer to her questions as quickly as possible, she suddenly knew an overwhelming desire to drag this confrontation out for as long as she could. She had just realised that this was probably going to be the very last conversation she ever had with Andreas. The last time she would be able to be with him and talk to him at all. After this, whatever his answer was, then they would go their separate ways. She would go home to England, to Macy and Daisy and some sort of life she would live there, and Andreas would stay here. And she would never, ever see him again.

The thought burned in her throat, closing it up so that she

had to struggle to breathe, concentrating so fiercely that she didn't hear Andreas speak even when he repeated the words more loudly.

'I—I'm sorry?'

'I said, would you like to sit down?'

Andreas gestured towards the settee with one of the wine glasses he held.

'Isn't it usual at this point to say—do I need to?' she managed, aiming for a joking tone.

But then she looked into Andreas' sombre, shadowed face and all trace of laughter, real or pretend, fled from her thoughts at once.

'Do I?' she asked on a note of anxiety.

'Sit down, Becca,' Andreas said and it was a command not a suggestion, one that had her slumping down onto the big leather settee without daring to protest or question any further.

'All right…'

Andreas sat opposite as he had before, placing both glasses of rich red wine on the table and pushing one towards her. Becca reached for hers, picked it up, then hesitated, looking down into the ruby-coloured liquid. She had the nasty feeling that if she tried to swallow it, her throat would constrict even more, choking her, and she would simply splutter the drink everywhere. With a faint sigh she set it down again and waited.

'So tell me about the baby. About Daisy.'

It was the chance she had wanted, that she had prayed for. But now that it was here she hardly knew where to begin.

But Andreas had used the baby's name. He'd called her Daisy. So surely he couldn't be going to turn his back on the little girl. Not when that seemed to mean that she was becoming a real person to him.

'I have a photograph—it's upstairs in my…'

She had been getting to her feet, anxious to go and fetch it, to show him her beautiful baby niece, but she stopped when he shook his head, sank back down into her seat instead.

'I want to hear about her from you.'

For a second Becca couldn't find the words, didn't know where to begin, but then she started hesitantly, and suddenly everything just came pouring out. How reluctant her sister had been to admit that she was having a baby. The way that Macy had neglected herself during her pregnancy…

'She's always been in danger of being anorexic and when she started getting bigger with the baby, she hated it. I tried to get her to eat, but she was always saying she was too fat. She never ate enough to keep herself alive, never mind let the baby grow healthy. Then she went into labour early—too early. Daisy was born prematurely…'

She choked off the words, unable to continue, staring in front of her with unfocused eyes as she remembered the tiny little scrap of humanity that the baby had been at that time.

'They managed to save her—but there are problems with her heart. We were told that the operation she needs isn't available in England—it's too new, too specialised. Before this babies like her just died—no one could do anything for them. But there's a surgeon in America who has been working wonders on tiny babies just like her. If we could just get him to operate on her.'

'And for that you need money.'

Becca could only nod silently, her heart too full for speech. Putting Daisy's plight into words like this had brought it home to her how desperate the situation was; made her remember just how fragile the little girl's life could be.

'And that is why you came to me?'

There was a note in his voice that she couldn't interpret, and his eyes were bleak as ice floes.

'I—I wrote to you about it,' she managed and Andreas nodded slowly.

'I remember that now—a letter that arrived just before the accident. Those days are still not clear.'

He frowned faintly, rubbing at his temples, obviously trying to recall things from before the car crash.

'The distant past is something I remember better. But I sent an answer, I believe.'

'Yes. You told me to get in touch with your solicitors—write down exactly what I needed and why and you would con—consider my request.'

That frown was back between Andreas' black brows, but it was more pronounced now.

'Then why are you here? Why didn't you just do that?'

'Because...' Becca began then broke off sharply as something Andreas had said a moment earlier hit home to her.

*Those days are still not clear... The distant past is something I remember better.*

Did he not remember that he had been asking for her? That was the one reason she was here. A reason that she had been forced to decide had just been Leander imagining things, because nothing in Andreas' behaviour seemed to fit with a moment like that.

But if he didn't remember...

'Because?' Andreas prompted harshly.

Leaning forward, Becca snatched up her glass of wine again and took an unwary gulp. It was enough to clear her head.

'Because I thought it was best to explain the situation to you face to face. You deserved that at least if you were going to help us.'

'But when you got here, you found that I didn't remember your letter—or you.'

'And so I let you think that we had never split up. I'm sorry,' Becca put in hastily and sincerely. 'I couldn't think of anything else to do.'

Andreas didn't seem to be listening. He was reaching into the pocket of his trousers, pulling out a folded piece of paper. He tossed it onto the table beside her wine glass.

'What's this?' Becca looked at him, puzzled.

'Open it and see.'

She picked up the paper with hands that shook, opened it with difficulty. But she couldn't make head or tail of the contents. Even when she held the document directly under the lamp, it still didn't make any sense and the words and figures on it—especially the figures—danced and blurred in front of her eyes.

'What is this?'

'Instructions to my bank—I faxed them just now. They will release the money—anything you need.'

'Anything I need...'

Becca couldn't believe that this was happening. Was it true. Had Andreas really said...?

'You're going to help?'

'I always said I would give you any money you needed.'

'Oh, thank you!'

It was hopelessly inadequate to express the way she felt. She wanted to dance for joy—she wanted to fling her arms around Andreas and kiss him...but a careful look into his dark, shuttered face made her rethink that idea hastily. Instead she reached out across the table and caught both of his hands in hers, holding them tightly.

'*Thank you*! Thank you so much!'

'My pleasure.'

The words meant one thing, but the expression in those glittering black eyes and the way that he pulled his hands from her grasp said something else completely and a lot of Becca's euphoria evaporated as he got up and moved away.

Of course—he was prepared to help Daisy, but not her. Though there was something he had said…

But before she could quite grasp what it was, Andreas had spoken again and his words pushed all other thoughts from her mind.

'So now you've got what you came for…'

How she wished that Andreas hadn't got to his feet because now he seemed to tower over her, dark and forbidding, as she registered what he had said.

She'd got what she'd come for and now he wanted her to leave. She'd been right that he couldn't let Daisy suffer for the division that had come between them, but his actions hadn't indicated any healing or even a hope of peace. He'd provided the money she needed; he wasn't offering her anything more.

'Of course.'

She stumbled to her feet in a rush, refusing to let the anguish in her heart show in her face. She might be falling apart inside at this speedy, cold-blooded dismissal, but outwardly she was determined to be as brisk and businesslike as possible.

'I'll leave at once. If you'd just give me time to pack, I'll be on my way. And if you call me a taxi—'

'No.'

It was hard and coldly savage, slashing into her words as she tried to get them out.

'No. That's not the way it's going to be.'

'It isn't?'

The sun was almost totally below the horizon now and the room so dark that she could scarcely see his face. But one last, lingering ray of light fell on the coldly glittering eyes, the start of his tightly clamped jaw. There was no yielding in him, no gentleness at all, and her heart quailed at the thought of just what he was about to say.

'You're not leaving.'

It was so unexpected that she almost laughed. But she caught back the betraying sound with an effort and managed to control her face so that the shocked astonishment she was feeling didn't show on it.

'Of course I am.'

She had to get home, tell Macy the wonderful news, get the hospital to put things in motion...

'You can't want me to stay.'

She blinked in astonishment as an autocratic flick of Andreas' hand brushed aside her protest in a second.

'That is where you are wrong, *agape mou*,' he told her with deadly intensity. 'I very much want you to stay.'

'But why...?'

'Oh, Becca, Becca...' Andreas reproved and the softness of his tone made an icy shiver crawl all the way down her spine. 'You are not so naïve that you have to ask that question. You know why I want you here, what I want from you.'

And of course she did.

'Sex,' she stated baldly and saw a frown draw his black, straight brows together.

'I prefer to call it passion.'

'You can call it what you like.'

The pain that was clawing at her heart made her voice harsh; the fight to hold back tears roughened it at the edges.

'But sex is what you mean and...'

Her voice failed her as a terrible truth dawned in her thoughts, the horror of it taking away all her strength.

'Is this about the money? Is this what you're demanding

in return for helping Daisy—your conditions for the loan? Is it what I have to do to ensure she gets the operation?'

She knew she was wrong as soon as she'd spoken. Even the shadows in the room couldn't disguise the way his head went back, the hiss of his breath between clenched teeth.

'What sort of a brute do you think I am?'

The vein of savage anger in Andreas' voice made her blood run cold. There was no room for possible doubt of his sincerity. But she didn't have the strength to take the words back, particularly not when his hand flashed out, clamped tight around her wrist and pulled her towards him with a rough, jerky movement.

'Your sister and her child, the money for the operation—money that is a gift, not a loan—all that is dealt with. You can get on the phone to your sister—to the hospital, tell them arrange everything—and then that is done. Finished. *This* is between you and me. And nothing is finished between the two of us.'

'But…' Becca tried to interject but Andreas ignored her weak attempt at speech.

'I let you go too easily the last time, and I've regretted it ever since. I've never been able to get you out of my mind. You've shadowed my days—haunted my dreams—and this afternoon in my bed reminded me of just why you have this effect on me. And it also told me that once would never be enough. I want so much more.'

Becca could only listen in dazed silence, struggling with the cruelly ambiguous feelings his words woke in her.

They should be complimentary. They should be what every woman dreamed of the man she loved saying to her. But she knew what he really meant and that destroyed any joy she might have wished she could find in what he was saying.

*Money I'll give you but nothing else,* he had flung at her, and now here he was, offering her nothing—nothing more than the cold-blooded passion he had for her, the purely physical need that he openly admitted was all he felt.

'And I know you feel it too. That's why I want you to stay. I'll make it worth your while. I'll give you anything you want—everything you want.'

*I have a reputation for generosity to my mistresses.* The words spoken outside by the pool—was it only a few hours ago?—came back to haunt her. And that was all she would be—his mistress. His wife in name but his mistress in reality. Because as his wife she should be loved, cherished—and she might hope to stay with him for life. As his mistress…

'How long?' she croaked out, her voice failing her. 'How long would you want me to stay?'

'For as long as it lasts. As long as it works. If we're both getting what we want out of this, then I don't see why it can't last…'

'Until we get each other out of our systems?'

Becca prayed that her falsely airy voice hid the agony that was squeezing her heart deep inside.

She would never get what she wanted out of this. Never. There was no hope of that, because what she wanted—what she longed for—was for Andreas to love her just as much as she loved him. And as she had given him her heart without hesitation or restraint in almost the first moment she had met him—and again here, when she had realised that she still adored him—there was no hope of that adoration ever being reciprocated.

*Money I'll give you—but nothing else. Not a damn thing else.*

And yet her body cried out to her to accept—her body and her weak, foolish heart that begged her to take this, take the little he was offering and accept it. It was better than nothing.

Better than having to turn now and walk away—knowing that
if she did so there was no hope that he would ever let her back
into his life again.

She couldn't do that. She had had to walk away from him
once, and the moment that he had slammed the door behind
her had almost killed her. She couldn't do it again.

*I married you for sex—for that and nothing else.*

And so when a weak, longing voice in the back of her mind
whispered that Leander had said that Andreas had asked for her
in the first few moments after he had regained consciousness—
he had asked for her and perhaps…she pushed it away and
made herself face the reality of what she was being offered.

And sex was all he wanted from her still. The thing that
was different now was that she no longer had any illusions.
She was no longer deceiving herself that Andreas loved her,
she knew exactly where she stood, and in that knowledge
was a desperate kind of strength.

In that moment the sun finally disappeared below the horizon,
and the last rays of light fled the room completely so that there
was only the small lamp in the corner to see by. And in the
darkness it was easy to hide the way she was really feeling.

In the darkness she could step forward and put herself
completely into Andreas' arms. With her face unseen, her
eyes and their betraying message hidden, she could put her
hand against the warm strength of his chest, whisper his name,
the single word, 'Yes,' and lift her face to his for his kiss.

And when his mouth came down hard on hers then all
thought stopped, only feeling began. And that was when
nothing else mattered. Only this man for whatever time she
might have with him. She would take that. And she would
never let herself dream of more.

## CHAPTER TWELVE

THE light of the full moon through the window made the bedroom almost as bright as day when Andreas finally gave up on any hope of sleeping and slid from the bed. Pulling on his jeans, he paused for a moment to look down at Becca's sleeping form, her body still curved as it had been when it had been pressed up against his, her face almost buried in the pillow.

She was completely out of it, lost in a world of total exhaustion, oblivious to anything. By rights he should feel that way too. The blazing passion between them had had full rein during the night, each hungry coming together more eager than the first, each tide of mounting pleasure stronger, each soaring, burning climax more mind-blowing than the one that had gone before. Never in his life had he known such pleasures, such delight in another person's body—in the gratification it could bring to every single one of his senses. And in the end it had been only exhaustion that had ended it. The exhaustion that had plunged Becca deep into the oblivion of sleep and left him lying awake and restless, staring at the ceiling as the moon rose high out in the bay.

At first he had had no idea why he too couldn't find the ease he needed in sleep. His body was sated, his clamouring senses quietened—for now anyway—but it was his mind that wouldn't let him rest.

It kept playing over and over again a snatch from the conversation that he had had with Becca days before. A set of words that were the reason for the way he was feeling, the cause of his unease.

'How long?' Becca had said. 'How long would you want me to stay?'

'For as long as it lasts. As long as it works. If we're both getting what we want out of this, then I don't see why it can't last…'

'Until we get each other out of our systems?'

The problem was, he reflected as he slipped out of the door and headed downstairs, he doubted that he would ever get Becca out of his system, no matter how hard he tried.

And God knew he had tried!

It had been a week now since she had agreed to stay, and every day it had seemed that instead of his appetite for her being blunted, it had grown until there wasn't a moment of his day, a single second in the night, even in his sleep, when his mind wasn't full of thoughts of her. It was worse than when he had thrown her out on the day of their wedding. At least then he had had no sight of her to remind him of how beautiful she was, no touch to bring home to him how fabulous she felt, no kiss to fill his mouth with her own essential taste. Instead, now she was always there, setting his senses on red alert, making him hungry again even in the moment of his greatest satisfaction.

If he had known that it would be like this, then just as he had told her to stay he might have hesitated, knowing that he was being a fool to himself to even consider it. He should have realised then that this would never be over, not for him; that he was only risking his peace of mind, his sanity, to take her back into his life again, knowing that one day she would walk out of it again.

She had been so determined to leave just as soon as she had the money she needed. She'd been on her feet and almost heading out the door when he had known that he could not let her go. He had wanted to have her, to hold her—and so he had damn nearly ordered her to stay.

'*To have and to hold from this day forward until death us do part...*' The lines from the wedding service haunted him as he made his way into his office, but he pushed them away, refusing to let them settle in his thoughts.

There was no till death us do part with Becca—she'd made that only too plain a year ago, when she had married him simply for his money while all the time conducting a passionate affair with Roy Stanton.

But now that Stanton was out of the picture...

Stanton *was* out of the picture, wasn't he? He had to be now that he had fathered Becca's sister's child.

Roy Stanton. The name tasted like acid in his mouth, making him want to spit as he unlocked the bottom drawer in his desk and yanked it open.

The file was still there. So often he had meant to take it out and shred it, burn the contents, but he had never quite managed to do it. Tonight he felt he could. He had to if he was to have a hope of moving forward.

Tossing it on the desk, he flung open the folder, flicked on a lamp and stared down at the photographs. It was a year since he had last seen them but they still had the effect of hitting him like a punch in his guts. The man he didn't know, though the investigator he had hired had told him that that was indeed Roy Stanton. And the woman's face was hidden so that she could be anyone. He had tried to convince himself that the investigator had been mistaken, that she was someone other than Becca. But the ring was the killer blow. There was no mistaking the ring on her hand.

It was the ring that had marked the betrothal of his great-grandmother to his great-grandfather, and had been passed down to him to give to his own future bride. He had put it on her finger himself when she had first agreed to marry him.

'What are those?'

The question came from behind him, making him start, spin round in shock. Becca stood in the doorway, her face pale, her eyes wide and her white cotton nightdress still floating round her from the effects of her movement, making her look like some ethereal spirit that haunted his home.

'Nothing important.'

His answer would be more convincing, Becca told herself, if it hadn't been so swift, so uneven, so blatantly obviously defensive in every way. Just the way he spoke and the look in those dark, dark eyes gave away the fact that whatever was in the file he had been looking at was very far from 'nothing important'.

'Just something I planned on shredding.'

'At three in the morning?'

'I couldn't sleep.'

'Neither could I—not after you left the bed.'

Of course, that wasn't the truth. She didn't know how long she'd lain there, alternately listening to Andreas tossing and turning, and knowing that he was lying far too still, trying so hard not to wake her. She didn't know what kept him from sleeping, and she'd been afraid to ask.

What if the week of total sensual indulgence had been enough for him? What if that was long enough to get her out of his system so that he was no longer getting what he had declared he wanted? Had his ardour cooled so fast that he was lying awake, wondering how to tell her?

When he'd crept from the room, she tried so hard to convince herself that wondering how to tell her wasn't Andreas' way. If he'd tired of her, he would tell her straight, no hesitation, no cushioning the blow. But even knowing that hadn't provided any comfort. In fact, it had only made things so much worse. If he wasn't trying to think of a way to tell her *that,* then what else was going through his mind to keep him on edge throughout the darkest hours?

She hadn't been able to stay where she was, with the space beside her in the bed growing colder with every second that passed. The feeling had reminded her too closely of the way she had felt when she had gone home after the disaster of their wedding day and had had to try to fall asleep in the bed that she had once shared with Andreas, knowing that she would never, ever sleep with him again. And so she had pulled on her nightdress and crept down the stairs after him.

But now she wished that she'd never done so. The look on Andreas' face, the sense of withdrawal that had hooded his eyes, tightened his jaw, worried her even more than his restlessness had done. There was something very wrong here and she couldn't begin to guess what.

And being in this room with him like this, in this incomprehensible mood, brought back unhappy memories of the way that he had confronted her here, on the night of their wedding.

'Then I should take you back there. I'm sure I can think of a way of helping us both to sleep.'

It was smoothly done. Almost convincing. But Becca's nerves were already on red alert, and, hypersensitive as she was to everything about Andreas, she caught the faint unevenness of his tone, the way his gaze had flicked to the file on the table and then away again.

There had been a file on the desk then too. In fact, she wasn't sure that it wasn't the same file.

'What *is* that?'

'Just business…'

His hand went out to close the file, but, alerted by his tone, Becca was there before him. Grabbing at it to get it from him, she sent it flying, the file, and the photographs it contained, falling wildly to the floor.

'Oh, I'm sorry…let me… Oh…'

On her knees beside the desk, she froze, staring down at the photographs in each hand.

'Who's this with Macy—and why do you have a picture of my sister?'

'Give them to me…'

Andreas had crouched down beside her, reaching for the pictures, but then he too froze, staring at her in blank confusion.

'What did you say?'

'Who's this?'

The look in his eyes made fear clutch at her heart. Just what was happening?

'No—the rest of it. "Who's this with…?"' he prompted.

'With Macy?'

Was that what he wanted? Or something else?

'If you want the man's name then I can't…'

'You don't recognise him?'

If the look in his eyes had been bad, then the raw urgency in his voice made her tremble.

'No—I—Andreas, what is this—what are you asking— what is this picture?'

He didn't answer but just held out his hand to take the photos from her. Then he gave her the other hand and helped her to her feet. All in total silence. When she was upright, he spread the photos on the desk and focused the beam of the lamp directly on them.

And waited.

This was important. No words needed to be used to tell her that. Andreas' silence and that wary, watching stance of his meant that she had to give the right answer. But what *was* the right answer?

There was only one way she could go with this.

The truth.

'I don't know what you want me to say, Andreas, but I'll tell you what I see.'

She touched the photograph lightly, her fingertip resting on the image of the slender, dark-haired woman.

'That's Macy—my half-sister—and that building behind her is where she has her flat. Or, rather, had her flat. Since she discovered she was expecting Daisy, she moved in with me and…'

Her voice trailed off as realisation dawned and suddenly she was looking at the picture again, knowing just when it had to have been taken.

'Are you telling me that that…' a wave of her hand indicated the man in the picture, small and slim and with a boyishly handsome but weak, self-indulgent-looking face '…is Roy Stanton?'

And that was the moment when she knew that something had really changed. Because when she looked into Andreas' eyes as she spoke the words she saw none of the anger, none of the hostility that her use of that name had always created, but instead there was a stunned expression in their darkness. And she could almost have sworn that there were new shadows under his eyes, giving them a bruised, exhausted look.

'How do you know that's your sister?' he asked now and his voice was so husky and raw that it made her wince. 'You can't see her face.'

'No, but I know the T-shirt she's wearing—and the shoes. Macy just *loves* the highest heels she can find. Of course, from the back she could almost be me but there's…'

The impact of what she'd said dried her throat, taking the words from her. In the half-light Andreas' face looked drawn and haggard, and that stunned look had given way to one of real horror.

'Is that what you thought, Andreas? Is that what—what someone told you?'

Once more she looked down at the photograph, seeing it this time as he might have seen it, if someone had told him that she was the woman in the picture.

A woman who had flung herself into the arms of the man with her. Into Roy Stanton's arms. A woman who had her own arms up and around his neck, one hand almost buried in the man's fair hair as she pressed her lips against his in an ardent, passionate kiss.

Almost buried. Because there was one finger that could be seen only too clearly. And on that finger was…

'She's wearing my ring!' Becca exclaimed.

'Forgive me.'

The words came together almost in unison, so that Andreas' voice clashed with hers in the same moment that she spoke. And for a second she couldn't quite register what he had said. But as she paused, a small, confused frown creasing the space between her brows, he spoke again, and this time there could be no doubt about what he said.

'Forgive me for ever doubting you. For thinking that she could be you. For believing you could be capable of marrying me for what you could get when really you were…'

He choked off the end of the sentence, too shaken to go any further.

'For… Is that what he told you I'd done? Oh, Andreas, I knew he was evil, but I never thought he'd take things that far.'

Her heart thudding in shock, she reached out and placed her hand over Andreas' where his rested still on the desktop. For a moment he showed no response, remaining absolutely still, but then his fingers curled around hers and held tight.

'Tell me,' he said softly.

'Just one thing first.'

She had to know. She had to ask. And his answer to this would mean so very much. It would mean all the world.

'Were you really going to shred these?'

Her answer was there in his eyes, in the expression on his stunning face. She didn't need any more but he gave it to her.

'Yes,' he said, his voice strong and firm this time, with no room for doubt in his tone. 'Yes, I was going to shred them—and burn them. And then—'

But Becca stopped him there, pressing a finger to his lips to keep back the rest of what he had been about to say.

'Later,' she whispered, looking deep into his eyes and willing him to believe there would be a 'later'. A much better, easier—please God—a happier time, when whatever he had been about to say could be spoken with no hesitation, no doubts.

'Let me tell you about my sister. The sister I should have told you about.'

She'd hurt him with that, Becca knew now. It had really stung that she hadn't trusted him enough. That she'd been so afraid of losing her one blood relative that she had kept

Macy's existence even from him. If they'd stayed together longer she would have told him.

And now she *could* tell him. There were none of the restrictions Macy had placed on her when they had first met. All the need for secrecy had gone now. So she could be as open as she wanted—as she needed to be.

So she launched into the story of how she had tried to find her birth mother, only to find that she had died just six months before. But there was a daughter, Becca's half-sister.

'Macy was barely nineteen then—and she was making a real mess of her life. She'd got in with a bad crowd, been in trouble with the law—she had a drug habit. I was so conscious of how good my life had been with my adoptive parents—how different from hers—so I begged her to let me help her. She promised me that if I'd stick by her—help her out—then she'd try to go straight. But to do that, she had to get away from everyone she knew. She made me promise not to tell anyone who she was or where she was. If I did, then she would just disappear and I'd never see her again. There was one man in particular—a man she owed money to. Lots of money.'

She paused, searching for the strength to go on, to bring that name into the conversation. But she didn't need to. Andreas was there before her.

'Roy Stanton.'

'Yes. They'd had a relationship—she was crazy about him, would do anything he asked. He'd got her hooked on drugs, and when she couldn't pay for more he loaned her the money she needed—but at a ruinous rate of interest. The debt had just mounted up and up, until there was no way at all that she could pay it.'

'So you paid it. Using the money I gave you.'

Becca nodded slowly.

'I'm sorry...' she began but Andreas stopped her urgent words with a gentle shake of his head.

'Don't be—it was the only thing that you could do. I understand. But oh, Becca, *agape mou,* did you never think what might happen? Rats like Roy Stanton are never satisfied, even when you've paid them off. They always want more. And if one source dries up, then they'll find another way to get the cash they want.'

Sorting through the photographs, he found another sheet of paper and held it out to her. Becca stared numbly at the photocopy of the cheque she had written to pay off Macy's debts.

'*He* told you—but you said...'

'I said I had you investigated and I did.' Andreas' tone was sombre, his eyes shadowed. 'I wanted to clear you for your own sake—so that there was never any need for doubt. But it wasn't the money that concerned me—you could have had all of that and more, and I wouldn't have given a damn. What I did care about was the rest...'

'The rest...' Becca echoed, her heart seeming to stop still in dread. Now they were coming to it and she wasn't at all sure that she wanted to know what was coming. 'What did he say, Andreas? Tell me!'

But even as she spoke she was hearing in her thoughts the words he'd said just a few moments earlier.

*For believing you could be capable of marrying me for what you could get when really you were...*

'He told you that we were lovers.'

She could see it all now. It was exactly the sort of thing that Roy Stanton was capable of. When she had paid off Macy's debts with the money Andreas had given her, he must have thought he was on to a good thing and moved from dealing drugs into a little—he believed—highly profitable blackmail. And it must have been Macy who had told him about Andreas.

'I think I know when this picture was taken,' she said slowly. 'In fact, it had to be then. I'd been visiting Macy and when I went to the bathroom I took my ring off when I washed my hands. By accident I left it on the side of the basin. I remember that when I went back to get it, Macy wouldn't let me in—she was flustered and obviously embarrassed. She obviously had someone in the flat, but I never thought...'

Becca's eyes focused on the picture of her sister. On the hand that was up and half-hidden in Stanton's hair.

'She was obsessed with him—could never say no to him. But she knew what I would think, so she tried to keep him hidden from me. When I asked about my ring—she took it off her finger! She'd found it in the bathroom and tried it on.'

'And that was the day that the investigator spotted them together.' Andreas' voice took up the story. 'I believed he'd done what I hoped for—that he'd found no evidence, cleared you completely. And so I married you and brought you here. I thought we were free of it all... The photographs were waiting when I went into my office.'

The horror of that moment was stamped so clearly on his strong features that Becca's heart twisted in a pale reflection of the pain he must have felt.

'And I thought it was just the money—Andreas, why didn't you show me the pictures then?'

She saw his answer in his eyes; in the pained glance he shot at the discarded photographs, with its dark echoes of what he had felt then, when he had first seen them.

'Because I couldn't bear to. I wanted you to think it was the money that mattered. I could not have shown you the photos. Could not have stood there while you looked at them and knew—as I believed you would know—that you'd ripped my heart out with your betrayal. With the thought that you loved someone else.'

Andreas shook his dark head in despair at his memories.

'I wanted you to leave thinking I hated you—not knowing how much I loved you, that in spite of everything I still loved you beyond bearing.'

'*Loved*?' Becca had to force herself to say it, to take the risk, though every nerve in her body clenched tight in fear that she might not hear what she wanted to hear most in all the world.

But Andreas didn't hesitate.

'*Love*,' he declared clearly and proudly, the emotion he was feeling burning bright in his eyes for her to see too. 'I still love you Becca, always will. I can do nothing else. You are in my heart, in my soul. You're part of me. With you I am complete. Without you I am only ever half a man.'

'And I love you, my darling. You're the other half of me.'

Her voice was breaking on the words and she couldn't have gone on. But she didn't need to. Andreas gathered her into his arms, holding her tight against him, and his kiss was all that she needed to know that nothing more had to be said. Or could be said. There were no words to describe the love that was in that kiss. The love that was hers now and for ever.

'So tell me,' she whispered when, safe in his arms, she finally got a chance to speak again. 'When you had shredded those photographs, what were you going to do?'

Andreas' smile was one of pure joy as he looked deep into her eyes.

'I was going to go upstairs and wake you, very gently. And then I was going to beg you to let us start again. I was going to tell you that I couldn't live without you. That even as I slammed the door behind you I knew that I'd made a terrible mistake—the worst mistake of my life—but I believed it was too late to take it back. That you'd been in my thoughts every day since you left. That you were the first person I thought of in the moments when I came round from the accident.'

'I know—Leander told me that you were asking for me. That's why I came here in the first place. Only by the time I got here, you'd lost your memory.'

'Perhaps that was some sort of defence mechanism. They always say that you don't lose your memory—you just don't want to recall what has happened. Perhaps I wanted to forget what a fool I'd been ever to let you go.'

Once more his arms tightened round her and his mouth came down on hers in a lingering, loving kiss that made Becca's senses spin in hungry delight.

'But never again,' Andreas whispered in her ear. 'I'm never going to let you go ever again. I want you with me all day every day so that I can spend the rest of my life loving you as you deserve to be loved. So that I can prove to you that you are the only woman for me.'

'And you are the only man I'll ever want,' Becca sighed. 'My husband, my soul mate, my love, for ever.'

\* \* \* \* \*

# SPECIAL EDITION

Life, Love and Family

*These contemporary romances will strike a chord with you
as heroines juggle life
and relationships on their way to true love.*

New York Times *bestselling author Linda Lael Miller
brings you a BRAND-NEW contemporary story
featuring her fan-favorite McKettrick family.*

Meg McKettrick is surprised to be reunited with her high
school flame, Brad O'Ballivan. After enjoying a career
as a country-and-western singer, Brad aches for a home
and family…and seeing Meg again makes him realize he
still loves her. But their pride manages to interfere with
love…until an unexpected matchmaker gets involved.

*Turn the page for a sneak preview of
THE McKETTRICK WAY by Linda Lael Miller
On sale November 20, wherever books are sold.*

Brad shoved the truck into gear and drove to the bottom of the hill, where the road forked. Turn left, and he'd be home in five minutes. Turn right, and he was headed for Indian Rock.

He had no damn business going to Indian Rock.

He had nothing to say to Meg McKettrick, and if he never set eyes on the woman again, it would be two weeks too soon.

He turned right.

He couldn't have said why.

He just drove straight to the Dixie Dog Drive-In.

Back in the day, he and Meg used to meet at the Dixie Dog, by tacit agreement, when either of them had been away. It had been some kind of universe thing, purely intuitive.

Passing familiar landmarks, Brad told himself he ought to turn around. The old days were gone. Things had ended badly between him and Meg anyhow, and she wasn't going to be at the Dixie Dog.

He kept driving.

He rounded a bend, and there was the Dixie Dog. Its big neon sign, a giant hot dog, was all lit up and going through its corny sequence—first it was covered in red squiggles of light, meant to suggest ketchup, and then yellow, for mustard.

Brad pulled into one of the slots next to a speaker, rolled down the truck window and ordered.

A girl roller-skated out with the order about five minutes later.

When she wheeled up to the driver's window, smiling, her eyes went wide with recognition, and she dropped the tray with a clatter.

Silently Brad swore. Damn if he hadn't forgotten he was a famous country singer.

The girl, a skinny thing wearing too much eye makeup, immediately started to cry. "I'm sorry!" she sobbed, squatting to gather up the mess.

"It's okay," Brad answered quietly, leaning to look down at her, catching a glimpse of her plastic name tag. "It's okay, Mandy. No harm done."

"I'll get you another dog and a shake right away, Mr. O'Ballivan!"

"Mandy?"

She stared up at him pitifully, sniffling. Thanks to the copious tears, most of the goop on her eyes had slid south. "Yes?"

"When you go back inside, could you not mention seeing me?"

"But you're Brad O'Ballivan!"

"Yeah," he answered, suppressing a sigh. "I know."

She rolled a little closer. "You wouldn't happen to have a picture you could autograph for me, would you?"

"Not with me," Brad answered.

"You could sign this napkin, though," Mandy said. "It's only got a little chocolate on the corner."

Brad took the paper napkin and her order pen, and scrawled his name. Handed both items back through the window.

She turned and whizzed back toward the side entrance to the Dixie Dog.

Brad waited, marveling that he hadn't considered incidents like this one before he'd decided to come back home. In retrospect, it seemed shortsighted, to say the least, but the truth was, he'd expected to be—Brad O'Ballivan.

Presently Mandy skated back out again, and this time she managed to hold on to the tray.

"I didn't tell a soul!" she whispered. "But Heather and Darlene *both* asked me why my mascara was all smeared." Efficiently she hooked the tray onto the bottom edge of the window.

Brad extended payment, but Mandy shook her head.

"The boss said it's on the house, since I dumped your first order on the ground."

He smiled. "Okay, then. Thanks."

Mandy retreated, and Brad was just reaching for the food when a bright red Blazer whipped into the space beside his. The driver's door sprang open, crashing into the metal speaker, and somebody got out in a hurry.

Something quickened inside Brad.

And in the next moment Meg McKettrick was standing practically on his running board, her blue eyes blazing.

Brad grinned. "I guess you're not over me after all," he said.

HARLEQUIN *Presents*

## In Bed WITH THE Boss

Chosen by him for business,
taken by him for pleasure…

A classic collection of office romances from
Harlequin Presents by your favorite authors

# ITALIAN BOSS,
# HOUSEKEEPER BRIDE
by Sharon Kendrick

Book #2687

Raffael needs a fiancée—and he's chosen his mousy
housekeeper Natasha! They have to pretend to be
engaged, but neither has to fake the explosive
attraction between them….

Available December 2007 wherever you buy books.

Look out for more sexy bosses,
coming soon in Harlequin Presents!

**www.eHarlequin.com**

HP12687

HARLEQUIN *Presents*

THE ROYAL HOUSE OF NIROLI

Always passionate, always proud.

**The richest royal family in the world—
a family united by blood and passion,
torn apart by deceit and desire.**

By royal decree, Harlequin Presents is delighted to bring you
The Royal House of Niroli. Step into the glamorous, enticing
world of the Nirolian Royal Family. As the king ails he
must find an heir…each month an exciting new installment
follows the epic search for the true Nirolian king. Eight heirs,
eight passionate romances, eight fantastic stories!

**Coming in December:**

# THE PRINCE'S FORBIDDEN VIRGIN
**by Robyn Donald**
### Book #2683

**Although Rosa Fierezza knows he's forbidden fruit,
she's under Max's spell. However, just when Rosa and
Max give up all hope of being together, the truth about
a scandal from the past may set them free….**

*Be sure not to miss the next book
in this fabulous series!*

**Coming in January:**
BRIDE BY ROYAL APPOINTMENT
by Raye Morgan  Book #2691
www.eHarlequin.com                    HP12683

# REQUEST YOUR FREE BOOKS!

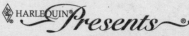 

## 2 FREE NOVELS
## PLUS 2
## FREE GIFTS!

**YES!** Please send me 2 FREE Harlequin Presents® novels and my 2 FREE gifts. After receiving them, if I don't wish to receive any more books, I can return the shipping statement marked "cancel." If I don't cancel, I will receive 6 brand-new novels every month and be billed just $3.80 per book in the U.S., or $4.47 per book in Canada, plus 25¢ shipping and handling per book and applicable taxes, if any*. That's a savings of close to 15% off the cover price! I understand that accepting the 2 free books and gifts places me under no obligation to buy anything. I can always return a shipment and cancel at any time. Even if I never buy another book from Harlequin, the two free books and gifts are mine to keep forever.

106 HDN EEXK   306 HDN EEXV

Name _____ (PLEASE PRINT) _____

Address _____ Apt. # _____

City _____ State/Prov. _____ Zip/Postal Code _____

Signature (if under 18, a parent or guardian must sign) _____

Mail to the **Harlequin Reader Service®:**
**IN U.S.A.:** P.O. Box 1867, Buffalo, NY 14240-1867
**IN CANADA:** P.O. Box 609, Fort Erie, Ontario L2A 5X3

Not valid to current Harlequin Presents subscribers.

**Want to try two free books from another line?**
**Call 1-800-873-8635 or visit www.morefreebooks.com.**

* Terms and prices subject to change without notice. NY residents add applicable sales tax. Canadian residents will be charged applicable provincial taxes and GST. This offer is limited to one order per household. All orders subject to approval. Credit or debit balances in a customer's account(s) may be offset by any other outstanding balance owed by or to the customer. Please allow 4 to 6 weeks for delivery.

**Your Privacy:** Harlequin is committed to protecting your privacy. Our Privacy Policy is available online at www.eHarlequin.com or upon request from the Reader Service. From time to time we make our lists of customers available to reputable firms who may have a product or service of interest to you. If you would prefer we not share your name and address, please check here. ☐

HP07

I ♥ HARLEQUIN® Presents

BROUGHT TO YOU BY FANS OF
**HARLEQUIN PRESENTS.**

We are its editors and authors
and biggest fans—and we'd
love to hear from YOU!

Subscribe today to our online blog at
**www.iheartpresents.com**

HPBLOG

## HARLEQUIN *Presents*

### RED HOT REVENGE

**There are times in a man's life…
when only seduction will settle old scores!**

This is

## Jennie Lucas's

debut book—be sure not to miss out on
a brilliant story from a fabulous new author!

# THE GREEK
# BILLIONAIRE'S
# BABY REVENGE

### Book #2690

When Nikos installed a new mistress, Anna fled.
Now Nikos is furious when he discovers Anna's
taken his son. He vows to possess Anna, and make
her learn who's boss!

Look out for more from Jennie coming soon!

**Available in December 2007
only from Harlequin Presents.**

Pick up our exciting series of revenge-filled romances—
they're recommended and red-hot!

**www.eHarlequin.com**          HP12690

# THE ITALIAN BILLIONAIRE'S CHRISTMAS MIRACLE
## by *Catherine Spencer*

### Book #: 2688

Domenico Silvaggio d'Avalos knows that beautiful,
unworldly Arlene Russell isn't mistress material—
but might she be suitable as his wife?

---

# HIS CHRISTMAS BRIDE
## by *Helen Brooks*

### Book #: 2689

Powerful billionaire Zak Hamilton understood
Blossom's vulnerabilities, and he had to have her.
What was more, he'd make sure he claimed her
as his bride—by Christmas!

Be sure not to miss out on these two fabulous
Christmas stories available December 2007,
brought to you by Harlequin Presents!

**www.eHarlequin.com**

HPCM1207

▼ *Silhouette*®

# SPECIAL EDITION™

brings you a heartwarming
new McKettrick's story from
*NEW YORK TIMES* BESTSELLING AUTHOR

# LINDA LAEL MILLER

## THE McKETTRICK *Way*

Meg McKettrick is surprised to be reunited
with her high school flame, Brad O'Ballivan,
who has returned home to his family's
neighboring ranch. After seeing Meg again,
Brad realizes he still loves her. But the pride
of both manage to interfere with love...until
an unexpected matchmaker gets involved.

—— McKettrick Women ——

*Available December wherever you buy books.*

**Visit Silhouette Books at www.eHarlequin.com** SSEIBC24867